USBORNE

ILLUSTRATED STORIES OF

HORSES
& PONIES

USBORNE
ILLUSTRATED STORIES OF

HORSES
& PONIES

Retold by
Rosie Dickins, Susanna Davidson,
Fiona Patchett, Rosie Hore
and Katie Daynes

Illustrated by
Yvonne Gilbert Nanos
and Natasha Kuricheva

Contents

The Talking Horse

Princess Lily loved to ride, and
the palace stables had many fine horses
for her to choose from. There were fiery
chestnuts, gleaming blacks and glossy
bays... but the horse she loved best
of all was a beautiful white mare
named Falada.

Falada was no ordinary horse. Her coat was the soft white of summer moonlight, her mane and tail were like spun silver – and there must have been a touch of magic in her, for she could talk. Lily and Falada were often to be seen galloping happily over the hills together, Lily's beautiful, nut-brown hair and Falada's silvery mane and tail streaming out behind them in the wind.

Now, Lily was engaged to marry the prince of a distant kingdom. Because their lands lay so far apart, they had not yet met. But they wrote each other long, loving letters and sent each other pictures and, when the prince invited her to visit, Lily set off happily.

The queen, who loved her daughter dearly, found her eyes brimming with tears as they said goodbye. Lily pulled out a handkerchief just in time to catch the drops – one, two, three –

that rolled down her mother's cheek. Then, with a last hug, they parted.

Lily rode out of the gates on Falada, followed by her maid, Grizela, on a sturdy little pony.

"Keep that handkerchief safe," said Falada, as they rode. "It will protect you – for a mother's love is a powerful charm."

"I will," said Lily. "Thank you." And she tucked the square of silk carefully into her sleeve.

It was a fine day and the palace was soon out of sight. The sun beat down and birds sang in the trees. Then there were no trees, and the road became hot and dusty. Watching her mistress ahead of her, Grizela began to scowl.

"Why should Lily be a princess, and ride a fancy horse, while I am only a servant?" she thought. "I'm just as good as her!" And she began to wonder if she might somehow take

Lily's place. "If only she didn't have that charm," she muttered, for she had heard Falada's words.

After a long while, they came to a fast-flowing stream. Lily turned to her maid. "Grizela, I am very thirsty. Please would you bring me some water?"

Grizela shrugged and tossed her dull brown hair. "Get it yourself," she said curtly.

Lily was startled, but too polite to argue. She climbed lightly down onto the bank and kneeled down to scoop up a handful of water. "Mmm." It was cool and delicious. She scooped up a second handful... and her handkerchief, trailing from her sleeve, brushed the surface of the water. Still thirsty, she reached out for a third handful…

The rushing water snatched at the silk and the handkerchief was gone.

"No," gasped Lily.

"Yes!" thought Grizela. "Now's my chance. Without that charm, Lily must do as I say."

Grizela jumped down and seized the princess roughly by the arm. "Listen," she hissed. "We are going to exchange dresses and horses, and you must say nothing to anyone. Promise me – or you'll be sorry!"

She looked so fierce that Lily turned pale and nodded, afraid to speak.

Falada whinnied softly: "If your mother only knew, her heart would break in two."

Grizela scowled at the horse. "And you'll say nothing either, you useless nag, if you know what's good for you."

So when they set off again, it was Grizela who rode Falada, dressed like a princess in royal silks and velvets – with the princess on the little pony, in a simple maid's dress, her beautiful nut-brown hair tied up under an old scarf, so that no one would recognize her.

When they finally arrived at the prince's high stone castle, the prince himself came out to greet them.

"Welcome, princess," he said, making a magnificent bow to Grizela. "And who are you?" he added, glancing at Lily, who was holding the horses' bridles. There was something about her that her ordinary clothes could not disguise. Lily, seeing his kind smile, longed to tell him everything. But she had made a promise, and could say nothing.

"Don't I know you from somewhere?" insisted the prince.

"No," snapped Grizela. "That's just my maid. Ignore her. She's so lazy, she's good for nothing except farm work."

"Well then, she can help Curley, our farm boy, look after the geese," replied the prince.

"And this old horse of mine can go and work on the farm too," added Grizela. "She acted up horribly on the way here, and I never want to see her again!"

In truth she was afraid Falada might speak up for her mistress, and wanted both of them as far out of the way as possible.

So the princess became a humble goose girl, and Falada a farm horse, pulling a wooden cart, while the maid feasted and danced, and did her best to impress the prince. She slept on soft, silken sheets in a huge golden four-poster bed,

while Lily slept on a scratchy straw mattress above the stable.

Each morning, Lily would climb down into Falada's stall. Then she would hug the horse's smooth, white neck and bury her face in that shining mane, until she felt better.

"If your mother only knew, her heart would break in two," Falada would whisper.

"At least we have each other," Lily would reply bravely. Then she would go with Curley, herding the geese out into the meadows.

Sometimes, Lily saw Falada again during the day, if the farmer drove the cart past the meadows. Then she would sigh, "Alas, Falada, toiling there!"

And the horse would reply softly, so softly the farmer and Curley could hardly hear, "Alas, princess, how ill you fare!"

That made Curley very curious.

"Who are you?" he asked, staring at his companion. "Why does that farm horse call you princess?"

But Lily just shook her head and smiled sadly. She had made a promise and she could not break it. Nor did she dare let anyone see her take down her hair, in case they recognized her. So when she wanted to comb it, she whispered secretly into the wind: "Blow, wind, blow! Make Curley's hat go!"

And the wind would whip Curley's hat away, so that he had to chase after it. By the time he returned, her hair would be combed and safely hidden away under the scarf once more. But although

Curley didn't see, someone else did. The prince was more and more suspicious of the visiting 'princess' and curious about her 'maid'.

Early one morning, he was riding past the farm as Lily embraced Falada.

"How strange," he thought. "That is surely a royal horse, and she loves it as a mistress, while the 'princess' does not."

Then he heard Falada speak. "A talking horse! That is stranger still," he thought. "And why should her mother's heart break in two?"

Determined to solve the mystery, he followed Lily at a distance and watched. He saw her speak to the wind and comb out her beautiful, nut-brown hair.

"There is some mischief here," he told himself. "This girl is the true princess, or I'm a goatherd."

He waited until Lily returned that evening,

and spoke to her in the kitchens as she came to get her supper. "Who are you?" he asked. "And why did your mistress send you away?"

Lily shook her head. She could not answer. Yet the prince felt more and more sure that he was right. "Why won't you speak?" he pleaded.

"I promised to tell no one," she admitted, "and I cannot break my word."

"Then I shall leave you," said the prince, "and you may whisper your troubles to that old iron stove in the corner. That would not be breaking your promise."

Lily nodded, waited until she was alone – then told the whole story.

The prince, meanwhile, was sitting just outside, with his ear pressed to the chimney. He heard everything, with growing outrage. As soon as Lily finished, he rushed in and took her in his arms. "My princess," he cried. "I knew it was you! Will you marry me?"

Lily looked up at him and smiled. "My prince," she sighed happily. "Yes."

"Then come with me," said the prince, leading her out of the kitchen into the great hall, where he gave orders for her to be dressed in royal robes, and for Falada to be brought back from the farm to the royal stables.

When Lily reappeared, she was wearing a rustling silk gown and a tiny crown of diamonds, which sparkled like starlight on top of her dark hair. The prince caught his breath, feeling suddenly shy.

Lily smiled and held out her hand, and they walked into dinner together.

Grizela was there already, gobbling pastries and marzipan cakes.

Lily looked so dazzling, Grizela didn't recognize her. She thought the prince had brought some foreign princess to meet her.

"Deli-i-ighted I'm sure," she drawled through a shower of crumbs, as the prince showed Lily to her chair.

When everyone had finished eating, the prince turned to Grizela.

"My dear," he said coolly. "What would you do if someone lied and deceived everyone like this?" And he went on to tell Lily's story. "What punishment would you suggest?" he asked when he had finished.

Grizela, unsuspecting, didn't hesitate. "I would make her tend the pigs," she laughed scornfully. "And sleep in the pigsty with them, but never take a bath!"

"So that shall be your punishment," said the prince. "Guards, take her away."

A few days later, the prince and princess were married under an arch of roses.

Lily's mother was there too, and wept once more – this time with tears of joy.

As for Falada, she tossed her silvery mane and gave the happy couple this blessing:

"Now at last your mother knows,
True happiness and love can grow."
And it did.

Bronze, Silver and Gold

Once upon a time there was a man with a meadow on the side of a mountain. Every year, he would cut down the grass and store it in his barn. But for the last two years, on midsummer's eve, just when the grass was at its thickest and greenest... something had come and eaten it all.

When the man came to visit his meadow, he found there was only the odd stalk left, sticking out of the ground. He turned to his three children and said, "This year, I want one of you to go to the barn and watch and wait and see what comes."

"May I go?" asked his daughter, Irene, the youngest of the three.

"Don't be ridiculous!" laughed her elder brothers. "You're just a little girl."

"I'll go," said the eldest boy, with a swagger. "I'll be sure to find out what it is."

So on midsummer's eve, he went to the barn and lay down on the straw-covered floor. He waited and waited and then, in the night, there came a noise like nothing he had ever heard before. The ground trembled, the walls shook and, in fear, the boy ran out of the barn, swearing he would never go back.

The next morning, the grass was gone again. There was only the odd stalk left, sticking out of the ground, and he realized something had come and eaten it all.

The next year, it was the turn of the second son. Like his brother before him, he set off with a swagger, vowing he'd find out what was eating the grass. But as night drew in and he lay down to rest, there again came the rumbling and the trembling, and the boy ran home as fast as his legs could carry him. In the morning, the grass was all but gone.

So the next year, the father turned to Irene and asked if she could go. Willingly, she agreed.

Her brothers mocked her. "You'll never find out what it is," they said. "You spend your life in the stables. All you're good for is looking after horses. How could you possibly succeed where we have failed?"

But Irene paid no attention to her mean-spirited brothers and, with a skip in her stride, she set off for the barn. As darkness drew in, she lay down to rest on a bed of straw and felt the ground tremble, just as her brothers had before her. The walls shook and the roof rattled so hard she was sure it was going to fall in. But she didn't run. Instead, she crept to the door and peered out. There, in the moonlight, chomping on the grass, was the finest, biggest, fattest horse she had ever seen. It shone russet-bronze in the moonlight, and by its side lay a bronze helmet, breastplate and shield to match.

"So *you've* been eating the grass," murmured Irene.

She crept out from the door and put on the helmet. It was a perfect fit. The gleaming breastplate and the shield, studded with jewels, followed next. Then, keeping her movements quiet and gentle, she swung herself onto the horse. As soon as she did so, the horse became gentle and biddable, and Irene rode it away to a place she had long kept secret.

"I'll call you Bronze," she said. "And I'll come back each day to care for you. There's plenty of grass for you to eat by day, and the best hay for when it gets cold at night."

When Irene returned home, her brothers were ready with their taunts and their sly laughter. "So how did you do?" they asked.

"Oh, there was nothing there," Irene replied airily. "I don't know why you made such a fuss.

I slept all night like a baby and the grass was still there in the morning."

The brothers gasped, but their father smiled.

"You won't be so lucky next year," jeered the eldest. "You had it easy compared to us."

The next midsummer's eve, Irene's brothers wouldn't dare go near the barn, but Irene went. This year, as she lay on the straw-covered floor, the ground shook and trembled more than ever. Irene steeled herself to look out of the door – and there was a horse chomping the grass, even larger and fatter than the one before. It shone silver in the moonlight, with a silvery mane and tail, and by its side lay a silver helmet, breastplate and shield to match.

As before, Irene put them on and, summoning her courage, she jumped onto the silver horse's back. It whinnied and paced, but she whispered calm words to quiet it.

"I'll call you Silver," she said, stroking its mane. Then she rode it away to her secret place. "I'll be back to care for you," she promised. "Here you have all the grass you could want to eat, and my beautiful Bronze for company."

The next year, on midsummer's eve, Irene went back to the barn once more. That night, the ground trembled and shook as never before. Irene was thrown from one side of the barn to the other and then everything went still.

She peered out of the door... There, in the moonlight, was the biggest horse of all. Its coat was burnished gold, as were its mane and tail, and by its side lay a gold helmet, breastplate and shield to match. Irene put them on and leaped onto the horse. It was so big and so strong, she could barely control it. It whinnied and reared, and she clung to its golden mane. But when she stroked its sleek neck to soothe it, the horse became calm. Then once again, she rode it away to her secret place.

"I'll call you Gold," she said. "You blaze as bright as the sun."

Soon after came news, trumpeted throughout the land, that the king was holding a contest, to see who could ride up the Hill of Glass. The king's son would stand at the top and the winner would be the first to pluck three golden apples from the prince's hand. In return, the winner could take his pick of the finest horse from the royal stables.

As soon as they heard the news, Irene's brothers were sure they could win the task.

"Of course *you* can't come!" they said, pointing at Irene and laughing. "A girl like you could never ride up the Hill of Glass."

Irene simply shrugged her shoulders and said nothing.

By the time the brothers arrived at the Hill of Glass, the crowds were thick with princes and knights, all trying to ride up the hill. But no sooner had they gone up a few steps than they slid down again, and no one could come near to the golden apples at the peak.

"It's impossible!" they complained to the king. "No one can do this."

Suddenly, there was a clattering of hooves and a knight in gleaming bronze came riding on a horse so fine, no one had ever seen the like of it before. The knight galloped up, up the hill. When he was a third of the way, the prince looked down from the peak, right into the knight's eyes, and gasped. At that moment, the knight turned the bronze horse around and began galloping down the glass slope, hooves clattering.

"Wait!" called the prince. And he threw down one of the golden apples. The knight caught it with a flourish, then galloped away, over the distant hills.

That night, all Irene's brothers could talk about was the knight in gleaming bronze.

"You should have seen him," they said. "Riding on his fine steed up the Hill of Glass!"

The next morning, Irene begged her brothers

to take her with them, but they only shook their heads and laughed at her.

They hurried off to the Hill of Glass and, as before, all the knights and princes tried to ride its steep slope, but none of them made it beyond the first few steps. They watched and they waited, but the rider in gleaming bronze was nowhere to be seen.

Then came a clattering of hooves and a knight appeared, dressed all in silver. This knight's horse was even bigger and finer than the one before, and its silver coat sparkled in the sunlight. The knight rode the horse up the hill. Up, up they went, until they were two-thirds of the way to the top. Then the knight turned the silver horse around and rode down again.

"Wait!" cried the prince. Again he threw an apple and down it flew. The knight caught it and galloped away, over the distant hills.

That night, Irene's brothers talked of nothing but the knight dressed in shining silver and how he had galloped up two-thirds of the hill.

"And tomorow will be the last day of the contest, for there is only one apple remaining."

"Please can I come with you?" begged Irene.

"No," scoffed her brothers. "You smell like the stables! We can't be seen with you."

Early the next morning, the brothers rushed to the Hill of Glass, hoping that the silver knight would be there again. But there was no sign of him. The prince stood at the top of the hill with one golden apple, and no one could reach him.

Then, just as everyone was giving up hope, there was the sound of thundering hooves. Over the horizon came a knight in burnished gold, riding such a dazzling golden horse, the crowds had to shield their eyes as if from the sun. It was the fastest steed that had ever been seen.

When they reached the Hill of Glass, the knight rode up it as if there were no hill at all. This time, he galloped straight to the top and plucked the last golden apple from the prince's hand. Then, before the prince could say a word, the golden knight whisked around and galloped down again.

"Come back!" cried the prince, finding his voice at last, but by then the knight was thundering past the crowds and out of sight.

That night, the king commanded all the knights and princes to come to his palace, and for the knight with the golden apples to come forward. "Then," he said, "we can celebrate his victory and award his prize."

As the king commanded, every knight and prince in the land came to the palace, but not one of them had the golden apples.

"We know *someone* has them," said the king, "for we saw him ride up the Hill of Glass with our own eyes." And he asked every man in the kingdom, farmers, carpenters, foresters all, to come to the palace.

One by one they came, empty handed.

At last, Irene's two brothers were presented to the king. They, too, had nothing to show. But the prince stared at them thoughtfully, as if he saw something familiar in their faces.

"Maybe it is not enough to see every man?" suggested the prince.

"What do you mean?" asked the king.

In reply, the prince turned to the brothers. "Do you have anyone else at home?"

"Only our sister, Irene," they said.

"Summon her to the palace at once," commanded the prince.

So the brothers sent for Irene to join them. She rode into the palace on her golden horse that shone brighter than the sun, with Bronze and Silver trotting behind her.

The onlookers gasped. Her brothers came close to fainting. "It can't be!" they muttered to each other.

"Do you have the golden apples?" asked the prince, with a smile.

"I do," replied Irene. "Here is the first, here is the second and here is the third." One by one, she pulled them from her pockets.

The king clapped her on the shoulder. "Never have I seen such fine horses," he said. "You rode better than all the knights and princes in the land. You have won the contest."

"You have also won my love," said the prince, bending down on one knee. "Irene, will you have me for your husband?"

"I will," Irene replied, smiling.

The wedding was held at the foot of the Hill of Glass. And for all we know they are there still, feasting and laughing and riding.

The Black Stallion

Prince Doros was lost in the forest. He had been out hunting when he had taken a wrong turn – and had quickly found himself deep among thorny thickets and dense undergrowth, with no sign of a path.

He wandered in the greeny gloom for a
whole day and night, branches and brambles
catching and scratching at his clothes. Finally,
tired and hungry, he stumbled into a clearing.
In the middle of the clearing loomed a tall stone
tower, with a wooden stable beyond it.

"I wonder who lives here," thought Doros,
walking up to a heavy wooden door. "Whoever
it is, I hope they can help me..." He lifted a
hand. *Rat-a-tat...* "Oh!"

The door had swung open to reveal a large,
round room, quite deserted. In the hearth, a log
fire hissed and crackled. In front of it stood a
table piled high with pastries and pies.

"Hello?" called Doros. "Is anyone there?"
His voice echoed around the stone walls, but
there was no reply.

Nervously, he walked over to the table. The
food smelled so good and he was so hungry, he

couldn't help himself. He picked up a pie and took a big, delicious bite...

KABOOM! A clap of thunder split the air, making the flames in the fireplace flicker. Doros blinked – and saw an old man in long, dark robes.

"Who steals from my table?" the man demanded fiercely.

"I'm s-sorry," stammered Doros, startled. "My name is Prince Doros. I am not a thief! I was just so hungry..."

The man frowned. "If you eat my food, you must pay me back by working for me."

"A prince always pays his debts," returned Doros proudly. "What would you have me do?"

"Keep this fire burning, and tend to the horse in my stable."

"That sounds easy enough," thought Doros, agreeing. He imagined he would work for a day or two, and then go on his way. He did not know that the man was a wicked magician, and did not mean to let him leave.

Doros set to work willingly. He built up the fire, until bright, hot flames leaped high above the glowing logs. Then he went outside and chopped splintery stacks of firewood, until his arms ached.

In the stable, he befriended the horse – a handsome black stallion named Solon, with the gift of human speech. He cleaned Solon's stall, and brought him soft hay and fresh water. Then he sang while he brushed the horse's silky coat and combed his long, flowing mane and tail. When he had finished, Solon gleamed darkly, like a starless sky at midnight.

But when the prince went to take his leave, the magician grumbled it wasn't enough. "Do you call that payment?" he sneered. "Get back and look after the fire!"

By nightfall, Doros was exhausted. He slumped in a corner and slept, while the flames in the hearth sank lower and lower...

The magician woke Doros in a fury. "You lazy layabout," he raged. "My fire has nearly gone out! Is this how you repay me? Get back to work at once!"

Doros did not know it, but the fire was the source of the magician's power. It had to be kept burning all day and all night, or his magic would fizzle out with it.

The next day, the magician made

Doros work twice as hard. The prince did his best, but the old man refused to be satisfied. Doros fed the fire, and chopped wood until he could hardly feel his arms. Then he went to tend the horse...

Solon whinnied sadly when he saw Doros. The prince's face was pale and there were dark shadows under his eyes.

"No good will come to you here," sighed the stallion. "My master the magician will work you to the bone and never let you go. He is a wicked man. But together, we can escape."

"How?" asked Doros thoughtfully. "If he is a magician, he will be hard to trick."

Solon nodded. "True," he said, "but I have a plan. First, you must bring my saddle and bridle – and be sure to bring the comb, whip and looking-glass you will find in the same cupboard. Hurry now!"

Doros did as the stallion asked and got the horse ready, buckling the soft leather straps of the tack around his sleek head and belly.

"Now," neighed Solon, tossing his head so the bridle jangled. "Jump up and let's be gone."

As soon as Doros was in the saddle, the black stallion galloped away, hooves drumming.

The horse was so swift, Doros felt as if they were flying. Wind whipped at their hair and the forest was soon a distant smudge on the horizon.

Behind them came a sound, like a faint echo of hoofbeats. When the prince glanced back, he saw a cloud of dust in the distance.

"The magician has magicked up a new mount," whinnied Solon. He galloped faster still, but the cloud was gaining on them.

The next time the prince looked back, he

could see the magician clearly. The old man's face was twisted with rage, and he was riding a strange, flame-red horse.

"Quick, throw the looking-glass down behind us," panted the stallion.

Doros fumbled in the saddlebag, then cast the mirror to the ground.

As soon as the glass touched the earth, it transformed into a vast lake of shining ice. When the flaming horse stepped onto the ice, clouds of steam billowed up around its hooves. The magician urged it forward, but the footing was treacherous. The red horse skidded and slipped and nearly fell, until the magician was forced to give up and ride the long way around.

All the while Solon raced on... but the magician's mount was faster than any earthly steed. Slowly but surely, he gained on them once more. When the prince turned, he could see the fiery glint in the red horse's eyes...

"Now, throw down the comb!" cried Solon. Doros did so. Where it fell, a forest sprang up. It was so dense and tangled, scarcely a bird could get through. As for the magician, he was obliged to dismount and hack a path slowly through the branches.

And still Solon raced on. Rather than tiring, he seemed to be galloping faster than ever. But even so, the prince soon heard hoofbeats thundering behind them.

"Can you see him?" whinnied Solon.

"Yes," replied the prince, glancing over his shoulder. The flame-red horse was easy to spot.

"Then throw down the whip," Solon told him. The prince did and – CRRRACK! The ground split open where it fell, and filled with a deep, fast-flowing river.

When the magician reached the riverbank,

he did not falter but urged his steed on. As the
water rose higher and higher around them, the
magical flames which had created the fiery horse
fizzed and sputtered, until at last they went out.
The horse vanished, leaving the magician in
mid-river. On he swam, an angry glint in his
eye... but just at that moment, the last log on his
fire burned out and his magic was finally
extinguished. With a cry, he sank beneath the
surface and was never heard from again.

At last, the midnight horse and the prince
were free. But their adventures together were not
over yet.

The black stallion had run so far and so fast,
all the places Doros knew had been left far
behind. The prince gazed around at the craggy,
unfamiliar landscape and sighed.

"What shall I do now?" he asked.

"Trust me and you shall do very well," replied Solon mysteriously.

Doros was too tired to ask any more, but let the stallion choose their path. They rode on for many hours, past rocky slopes and rushing streams, until a magnificent castle came into sight. At last, Solon stopped.

"Three princesses live there, with their father the king," he told the prince. "You must knock at the gate and ask for work. But don't tell anyone you are a prince, or mention me."

"They wouldn't believe I was a prince anyway," sighed Doros, glancing down at his dirty, torn tunic and work-roughened hands.

So Doros walked up to the castle alone, leaving the stallion hidden in a cave nearby, and got a job sweeping leaves in the gardens. In exchange, he received a penny a day and meals – though he never ate all his food, but always kept half for his horse, and scattered the crumbs for the birds.

No one paid much notice to the newcomer, except the youngest princess, Eleni. She watched him from her window and wondered who he was. She thought him very handsome and knew him to be kind, for she saw him feeding the birds.

Soon after Doros arrived, there was a competition. Princes came from far and wide to take part. Each princess was to throw a silver apple, and whoever caught it would be her husband.

The two eldest princesses

smiled and threw their apples to two noble princes. Eleni hesitated, then threw her apple high above the heads of her royal suitors... *Thump!* It landed at the feet of the lowly leaf-sweeper.

Startled, Doros glanced around but there was no one else near. So he picked up the apple and brought it back to Eleni. As he handed it to her with a deep bow, their fingers touched and his heart gave a jolt.

"I wish *I* could be her suitor," he thought, as she thanked him with a glowing smile.

"Of course that was a mistake," blustered the king. "Throw again!"

"No, Father," replied Eleni quietly. "He had the apple, I shall marry him – if he is willing?"

"Yes, princess," cried Doros gallantly, hardly able to believe his good fortune.

The king frowned. "So be it," he snapped.

So the eldest princesses married their princes and lived in luxury, while the youngest married a servant and made her home in a gardener's hut. Yet she and Doros were blissfully happy together. They lived peacefully – until one day, news came of an invading army.

The king summoned the princes who had married his eldest daughters, and gave orders to saddle his finest battle chargers.

"May I come with you?" asked Doros.

The princes laughed scornfully.

The king shook his head. "You're a gardener!" he snorted. "What do you know of battle? You can't even ride a horse!"

He and the princes cantered off at the head of his army, in a dazzle of dancing hooves, tossing manes and swishing tails.

Doros was determined not to be left behind. As soon as the king was out of sight, he made haste to Solon's cave and told him everything.

"Hrrrumph," snorted the stallion, when he heard about the invasion. "To battle!" He struck the cave floor with a powerful hoof.

Crack! The rock split apart, revealing a knight's outfit of polished gold, with a shining silver sword. Doros smiled.

A few minutes later, Doros galloped off after the army on a magnificent midnight-black steed, his new golden suit and helmet flashing in the sun.

With his face hidden by the helmet, no one recognized Doros. He fought like a lion, his silver sword flashing. Solon was equally brave, crashing fearlessly through the fray.

The king's forces had been struggling, but as soon as Doros appeared their fortunes turned. After a few more skirmishes, the enemy fled.

"Hurrah for the golden knight!" cried the king in triumph.

"Hurrah! Hurrah!" echoed his grateful army.

Doros lifted his arm in acknowledgement – and several drops of bright-red blood splashed onto the ground.

"You're wounded!" exclaimed the king in concern, pulling out a silk handkerchief to serve as a bandage. "Who *are* you?" he asked,

as he wrapped the royal handkerchief carefully around the cut himself.

The stranger did not answer. He only shook his head mutely and galloped away.

That night, there was a victory banquet at the castle. All the talk was of the mysterious hero who had come to the king's aid.

"I've never seen anything like it," said the king admiringly. "He was completely fearless. Dressed all in gold, on a black charger... it was a magnificent sight."

"I wish *we* could have seen him," sighed the eldest princesses.

Meanwhile, Doros was sound asleep on the straw mattress in his hut. He was so worn out, he didn't even stir when his wife came in.

"Oh no," thought Eleni, seeing a bandage on his arm. She leaned down to inspect the wound – and gasped.

There, on the strip of silk, was a royal crown. It looked very familiar...

"That is *Father's* handkerchief!" she realized. "THIS is the hero everyone is talking about!"

Gently she kissed her sleeping husband, then went to tell the king...

Amazed and delighted by his son-in-law's courage, the king gave him a palace and half his kingdom as a reward, and built a beautiful new stable for Solon.

Across the land, the celebrations and laughter lasted for weeks, and they all lived together happily – the prince, the princess and the magical stallion with the coat like the midnight sky – for the rest of their days.

The Little Humpbacked Pony

Once upon a time, there were three sisters who lived together on a farm. Lena and Nena, the eldest, were sensible and dull, and truth to tell rather selfish. The youngest, Yana, always had her head in the clouds and a different way of doing things, so Lena and Nena thought she was very silly.

If it rained, Yana would hang out the washing in the yard.

"But it won't dry!" mocked Lena.

"No, but it will be rinsed very clean," Yana answered quietly.

If the sun was blazing, Yana would build up the fire and bake bread.

"You're making the house hotter!" moaned Nena, fanning herself.

"Sorry!" said Yana. "It was so hot already, I thought you wouldn't notice."

Then Lena and Nena would roll their eyes and sigh, "Foolish Yana!"

At one end of the farm lay a large apple orchard. But this year, they had had hardly any fruit. Night after night, someone was stealing the sweetest apples. Lena and Nena tried watching over the trees, but the cold bit their fingers and numbed their noses, until they took shelter in the barn – and so they saw nothing.

Then it was Yana's turn. She sat among the trees, careless of the chill. An icy wind blew in from the north, but she scarcely noticed. She was too busy smiling at the stars.

Then, she heard the noise of hooves. She turned and saw a milk-white mare through the trees. Her mane and tail fell in golden ringlets almost to the ground. As Yana watched, the mare stretched up and bit into a ripe, red apple.

"So you're the thief!" muttered Yana.

Slowly, quietly, she edged closer to the mare – who was too busy munching and crunching

to notice. When she was close enough, she leaped for the mare's back. At the last moment, the mare heard her and turned to flee, so Yana landed the wrong way, facing the mare's golden tail. There was no time to do anything but cling on as the mare bucked and twisted, trying to throw Yana to the ground.

Suddenly, the mare dashed between the trees and leaped over the wall, to race across the hills beyond. Yana kept her fingers twisted tightly around the mare's tail and tried not to think about falling off.

Finally, the mare came to a halt, her sides heaving and her mouth flecked with foam. She craned her beautiful white head around to gaze at Yana. Then, to Yana's utter astonishment, she spoke.

"Please, let me go!" she begged. "In exchange, I will bring you three foals. Two will be handsome colts, as black as night, with golden manes and tails. The third will be a humpbacked pony – little, but with a big heart. They will bring you great good fortune, but you must never part with the pony. Promise me!"

"I promise," said Yana sincerely, releasing her grip and sliding to the ground.

The mare whinnied her thanks, then turned and trotted quietly into the dark. Yana watched until she vanished from sight, then turned and trudged home alone. It was a long walk and she fell into bed, exhausted but amazed.

She was woken by her sisters shaking her.

"You were supposed to keep watch!" Lena cried. "But here you are, in bed. Lazybones!"

"I DID keep watch," insisted Yana, yawning. "I caught the thief!"

"So what happened?" demanded Nena.

Rubbing the sleep from her eyes, Yana told her sisters everything that had happened. When she finished, they rolled their eyes.

"Foolish girl," Lena sighed. "You must have been dreaming."

Yet the next day, Yana found three foals in the furthest field. Two were darkest ebony, with bright gold manes and tails. The third was a curious creature, so small it scarcely reached her knees. It had a dun-brown coat, long ears like a donkey and a round, humped back.

"Well look at you," said Yana fondly, bending down to rub its nose. At her touch, it clapped its ears together and frisked around happily, stamping its little hooves for joy.

When Lena and Nena saw the foals, they realized Yana had been telling the truth. But they weren't very impressed. "You'll have to look after those creatures yourself," Lena said sharply. "Nena and I have enough to do already!"

So Yana cared for the foals alone. She brushed their coats and braided their manes, and fed them the finest oats and hay. Each night, she brought them into the barn; each morning, she let them out to roll in the dew.

The two black foals grew into tall black stallions, with proudly arched necks and long, golden manes and tails – horses worthy of the tsar himself. The little humpbacked foal grew into... a little humpbacked pony. But he was a merry, affectionate creature and Yana loved him dearly. She confided all her thoughts to him and, sometimes, she was almost sure he understood her.

So things went until one day, Lena and Nena happened to walk past the field and noticed the horses. "Look at them now," said Nena. "Those black stallions must be worth an absolute fortune!"

"We should take them and sell them," said Lena. "It's not fair of Yana to keep them to herself. The farm belongs to all of us."

"Yes – we can leave her that little humpbacked creature," laughed Nena. "Only Yana could want such an ugly animal!"

The next morning, they rose before the sun and set off for the local horse fair, so as to be well on their way before Yana woke.

When Yana went to let the horses out, she found only the little humpbacked pony.

"Where are your brothers?" she gasped in shock. "Have they been stolen? My poor stallions, what shall I do…"

She was even more shocked when the pony answered: "Your sisters have taken them to sell. But never fear! Jump on my back and we will soon catch up with them."

Yana sat carefully on his back, bending her legs so her feet wouldn't trail on the ground.

"Now, hold onto my ears so you don't fall..." And with that, the little humpbacked pony reared up and was off – so swiftly, the wind made his ears flap and Yana's eyes water.

She blinked to clear them, and saw they were halfway down the road to town.

She blinked again – and there were her sisters, each leading a handsome black stallion and talking carelessly about what they would do with their new-found wealth.

"Why have you taken my horses?" asked Yana simply.

The sisters exchanged glances.

"Er... we needed money for, um, things on the farm," said Lena.

"Yes," agreed Nena hastily. "We didn't want to worry you, but we had to sell *something* – and these fine horses are the best solution."

Lena nodded vigorously. "Yes, beasts like these should be worth a hundred gold coins apiece!"

"In that case, I will come and help you to sell them," said Yana.

"Are you sure?" asked Lena, reluctantly. "You don't know anything about selling."

"Then I will learn," replied Yana simply.

So the three sisters continued on their way together – Lena and Nena racking their brains for a way to be rid of Yana.

As they passed through a forest, they spotted something bright among the trees. It flickered red and gold, like flame...

"Look," said Lena. "Someone has left a fire burning over there."

"Oh no," exclaimed Nena. "If it spreads, the whole forest could burn to the ground. Someone should put it out."

"Not you or me," said Lena. "We can't be late for the fair!"

"I'll go," offered Yana.

"Thank you," said her sisters quickly. And they hastened off, while Yana and the humpbacked pony turned aside.

As they drew closer to the flame, it grew even brighter – but there was no crackle of burning wood, no smoke or sparks...

"How strange," thought Yana.

Then she spotted it. "Oh!" There, caught on a branch, was a long, golden-red feather. It shone as brightly as any flame. Yana reached up wonderingly... Although fiery to look at, it was soft and warm to touch. "It's beautiful!"

She was about to tuck it in her hair when the humpbacked pony spoke.

"Take care," he warned. "That is a firebird feather. It will bring you bad luck if anyone sees it." So Yana slipped it inside her jacket instead.

Then they galloped back to the sisters, catching up with them on the outskirts of the town. People thronged the streets leading to the horse fair, riding or leading all kinds of horses – pretty ponies, sturdy workhorses, high-stepping carriage horses...

The stallions caused a huge commotion. No one had ever seen such fine animals before. A crowd quickly gathered around them, arguing and bidding to buy. There was so much noise, the tsar himself heard it from his palace and drove out in his carriage, to find out the cause.

As soon as the tsar saw the stallions, he knew he had to have them – for the tsar always had to have the best of everything. "Such horses belong in a royal stable," he declared. "I shall give you a sackful of gold for each."

Lena and Nena tried not to grin too widely.

"Very well, your majesty," they said.

So the stallions were sold. Yana patted their arched ebony necks and handed their lead-ropes to the royal groom. "You will take good care of them?" she whispered sadly.

"Of course," huffed the groom. "The tsar keeps not only the best horses, but the best stables and the best groom." Then he tried to lead them away – but they refused to budge.

"Come on," coaxed the groom, holding out

a sugar lump. The stallions eyed the sugar and
snorted. "Come on!" he repeated, tugging the
ropes. The stallions bared their teeth. "NOW!"
he snapped, tugging harder.

In reply, the stallions reared up, gold manes
and tails flashing. They yanked the lead-ropes
free and trotted over to Yana. Then they stood
meekly while she patted their noses and
gathered up the trailing ropes again.

"I see we need a
new groom for these
horses," said the
tsar, watching.

"You're hired," he told Yana.

So Yana gave her sisters the gold, and bid them take care of themselves and the farm. Then she led the stallions to the tsar's stables, followed by the little humpbacked pony.

Each morning, she let her charges out to roll in the dew-spangled grass. Each evening, she brought them in, and fed them honey and oats and wheat. She brushed their coats and braided their manes. On high days and holidays, the stallions pulled the tsar's coach through the streets to cheering crowds. And so they all lived happily – for a while.

The tsar was delighted with his new horses and his new groom. But his old groom was less happy. He hated Yana. "Why should *she* get all the credit?" he muttered to himself. "She's just an upstart girl! I'm the real groom, I've always looked after the tsar's horses." And he kept a close watch on Yana, hoping for a chance to get her into trouble.

It wasn't easy – Yana looked after the horses too well. But one gloomy winter day, he saw a strange glow coming from their stable. He crept closer, and peered through a chink. Inside, Yana was grooming her charges by the light of... "A feather?" thought the groom, astonished. Fiery red or flaming gold, the feather seemed to create its own light.

When Yana had finished, she hid the feather under an old sack – but the groom saw where. As soon as she left, he crept in, snatched it and took it to the tsar.

"What bird did this come from?" wondered the tsar, turning it over in his hand, golden light pouring through his fingers. "It must be a wonderful creature. I long to see one!"

"The mighty tsar deserves no less," said the old groom silkily.

The tsar nodded. "Who will bring me one?"

"Yana," said the groom promptly. "It was she who had the feather."

"Bring her to me!" ordered the tsar.

Yana was horrified when she saw the tsar holding the feather. "It's a firebird feather," she admitted. "But I've never seen the bird! I found the feather in the woods."

The old groom smiled slyly. "Oh, but I heard you just yesterday boasting how you could catch a firebird."

The tsar scowled. "So my new groom is a liar!" he said curtly. "You should be locked in the darkest dungeon – but bring me a firebird and I will forgive you."

Yana bowed and hurried away. Back in the stable, she poured out her troubles to the little humpbacked pony.

"What shall I do?" she sighed. "I can't bring him a firebird, I've never even seen one! No one has. I wish I'd never found that feather."

The humpbacked pony nuzzled her softly. "I can help," he said. "The firebirds live on the Silver Mountain, a whole flock of them. No human has ever been there before – but I have and I will take you there. Listen carefully, you must pack a strong sack, a flask of wine and a bag of grain..."

The next day, Yana and the little pony set out at dawn, a large bag of grain and flask of wine wrapped in a sack and tied to her saddle. They rode swiftly, the pony's ears blowing back in the wind. After seven days and seven nights, they reached a forest of dark, tangled trees.

"Beyond those trees lies the Silver Mountain," said the humpbacked pony.

"There's no path!" exclaimed Yana.

"We must make our own," replied the pony.

So Yana dismounted and together they began pushing their way between branches and brambles. At last the trees thinned and Yana glimpsed a flash of silver... "The mountain!" she cried. It gleamed brightly in the distance, its peak so high it was lost among the clouds. After another day and night, they reached its foot.

"But there's no path," said Yana again, looking at the sheer silver slope.

"I don't need one," said the pony, tossing his head so his ears flapped. "Jump on!"

As soon as he felt Yana's arms around his neck he leaped forward, surefooted and swift. Higher and higher he climbed, until Yana didn't dare look down.

Almost at the very top was a ledge where a spring gurgled up, filling a tiny silver pool, before rushing away down the mountain in glittering waterfalls. Around the pool grew emerald moss, dotted with jewel-bright flowers. It was a beautiful place.

"The firebirds come here to drink every morning at dawn," said the pony. "Listen. Soak the grain in the wine, scatter it around the spring – then hide behind this rock. When the firebirds eat the grain, they will become sleepy. Creep out and quickly catch hold of the nearest, and wrap it in the sack before it flies away."

So Yana soaked and scattered the grain, and hid. Then she waited... Just as the sun broke the horizon, a flash of gold caught her eye. The flash became a blaze as dozens of firebirds swooped down through the clouds, to land on the ledge. Light shone from their flaming

red-gold feathers, making the half-light of dawn as bright as midday.

The birds began pecking greedily at the grain, squawking with pleasure. As they ate, their eyelids began to droop. One by one, they tucked their heads under their wings and settled down to sleep.

"Now!" thought Yana. As quietly as she could, she stole forward, stretched out her hand... and closed it around a slumbering bird.

Immediately the firebird roused. It began fluttering and flapping, and trying to pull free. Its frantic squawks woke the other firebirds, who took to the air with a loud whirr of red-and-gold wings, filling the air with dazzling light. But Yana held on tight.

The bird was surprisingly warm to touch – as if the fiery light it gave off really was some kind of flame.

"Quick, put it in the sack before it burns your hand," warned the humpbacked pony.

So Yana did. "There, there, little bird," she said soothingly. "I'm not going to hurt you, only bring you to the tsar. You will be a worthy addition to his court."

Then she gently tied the sack behind the saddle, and they rode back. The humpbacked pony's ears flapped in the wind as he trotted eagerly back down the mountain and through the tangled forest...

By the time they arrived, the tsar was brimming with impatience. "Come along!" he cried, as soon as he saw Yana. "Where's this fabulous bird?"

In reply, Yana opened the sack. The firebird darted out, its radiant plumage flooding the palace with flickering golden light. It swooped and circled, and came to rest on the back of the throne. The tsar stroked its feathers. "What a magnificent bird!" he said happily.

The old groom scowled. "Still, I *will* be rid of Yana," he thought bitterly. "If not this time, then next. I'll just have to wait a little longer."

The tsar was very proud of the firebird. He showed it off to every visitor, enjoying their gasps of admiration – until one day, a stranger from the ends of the earth smiled coolly and said, "Your bird is indeed very beautiful, but not as beautiful as the Fire-Maiden."

"Who is she?" demanded the tsar, offended.

"Why, the sister of the sun," answered the stranger. "She sails the ocean in a golden boat, and her long, golden hair is as bright as the sun's rays."

"I must see her," sighed the tsar. "It's time

I found a wife – why not this Fire-Maiden?"

"It won't be easy," warned the stranger. "She comes ashore only twice a year."

"I'll send Yana," decided the tsar. "If she can find me a firebird, she can find the Fire-Maiden. If she doesn't, I'll lock her up!"

Yana was filled with dismay. "I don't know how to find the Fire-Maiden!" she whispered to the humpbacked pony. "What shall I do?"

"Never fear," said the pony. "I will help you. But first, we will need a tent of gold brocade, and a golden tray of honey cakes."

The next day, they set off with the tent and tray of cakes in a large saddlebag. The humpbacked pony covered the ground swiftly, his ears flapping in the wind. After seven days and nights, they reached the sea. Golden sand stretched down to sparkling sapphire water.

"This is the shore at the end of the world,"

said the pony.

Yana shielded her eyes and gazed out across the waves... "I can't see a boat," she sighed.

"No," said the pony. "But set up the tent and lay out the cakes." So Yana did. "Now we must wait," the pony told her.

As the sun began to sink below the horizon, Yana spotted a golden glimmer in the distance. It came closer and closer, until she saw a golden boat. "The Fire-Maiden," she breathed.

The boat gleamed brightly – but not as brightly as the maiden's hair. Its golden strands rippled with a fiery glow, bringing warmth and light to the shore, even as the sun sank.

As the boat drew closer, Yana heard a sweet sound. The maiden was singing as she plucked a silver harp. When the boat reached the sand, she sprang lightly ashore and came to peer curiously into the tent.

"How pretty," she said in a musical voice. Then she glimpsed the honey-cakes. "How delicious!" She was about to take one when Yana stepped forwards. The maiden froze, her eyes wide.

"Dear maiden, do not be afraid," said Yana. "I have been sent to bring you to the tsar."

"I do not wish to go," said the maiden simply. "I prefer to sail across the ocean, feeling the seaspray and breathing the salt air."

"Please," begged Yana. "He told me that

he would throw me in his dungeons if I returned without you."

"He has no right to do that!" exclaimed the Fire-Maiden crossly. "Well. Maybe I should come and teach him so."

So the two rode back together on the little humpbacked pony. As they journeyed, they talked and laughed together, and became the very best of friends.

The tsar was delighted to meet the maiden. He looked her up and down greedily. "If I marry her, I shall be the envy of every other king," he thought. And he proposed to her on the spot.

"Ah tsar, you flatter me," answered the maiden. "But I fear I could never marry someone as old as you! Your hair is as white as mine is golden."

"I cannot turn back time," said the tsar. "But

think carefully. If you marry me, you will be a queen and very rich."

"Even so," said the maiden, shaking her head firmly.

But the tsar persisted – until eventually, the maiden said, "Well... it so happens that there may be a way. Did you know, if you bathe in boiling milk, with the right herbs, you can be made young again?"

The tsar immediately ordered a cauldron of boiling milk and fragrant herbs, just as the Fire-Maiden instructed. Yet when he looked into the steaming pot, he felt a nagging doubt. "What if this doesn't work? I need someone else to try it first. Fetch Yana!"

So Yana came, with the little humpbacked pony trotting at her heels. She trembled when she saw the boiling cauldron.

"Fear not," whispered the pony. "Allow me to

touch the milk and all will be well."

Yana watched nervously as he dipped his nose into the scalding milk, then lifted it up again unscathed. Taking heart, she stepped in. To her surprise, it felt no hotter than a warm bath. Steam rose around her, hiding her from view. Then she stepped out again, and heard the onlookers gasp.

Yana was now as radiant as the Fire-Maiden, and her golden hair shone with its own light.

"Amazing!" cried the tsar, hurrying over. He jumped right in – *splosh!* Then he leaped out again, with a yelp of pain. "Owwww!" he cried, hopping from foot to scalded foot. "What's wrong – why won't it work for me?"

The Fire-Maiden looked at him coolly. "You want too much and never think of others. I will never marry you."

The tsar frowned. Yana waited for his anger

to explode. But perhaps some magic had worked on him after all, because then he nodded. "I-I suppose you're right," he said slowly. "I'm sorry." As he spoke the unfamiliar word, the pain in his feet faded.

The Fire-Maiden smiled and turned to Yana.

"Now I must leave," she said. "Will you come with me, Fire-Sister?"

"Oh yes!" said Yana happily. So she and the Fire-Maiden rode the little humpbacked pony back to the golden shore, this time followed by two black stallions. And they all lived happily in freedom together, beside the sapphire sea.

The Kelpie

Far away to the north, on the shores of Loch Ness, lived a man and his wife and their young daughter. They were poor people, with a small cottage and a tiny patch of land that swept down to the shores of the loch. Food was scarce, the winters were long and their fear of starvation was real.

One spring, the man said to his wife, "I'm too old to till the soil this year and our daughter is still too young."

"Then we'll starve," sobbed the woman. "If we can't till our soil, we can't plant our crops…"

But the man pointed to the shores of the loch. "I've seen a horse down there, splashing in the shallows," he said. "It's black as midnight and it comes when the moon is full and the water gleams like silver. If I can only catch it, we can use it to till our land."

But the woman cried out and clung to him. "Don't go near it," she pleaded. "Haven't you heard the tale of the water-horse? It's no normal beast but a kelpie, with a spirit that's as bad as it's wild."

"Nonsense," the man replied.

His wife held onto him still. "No rope can control it, only a bridle of iron. And when you're

on its back, you're trapped. It'll ride you into the freezing waters and from there, you'll never come back."

The man saw the fear in his wife's face but he was driven by the growl of hunger and the sight of his untended land. So as soon as the moon was full once more and the waters of the loch turned silver, he went out in search of the water-horse.

He found it standing in the shallows, black as midnight and as strong as waves in a storm. He took out a rope for a bridle and leaped on the horse's back. No sooner was he astride, than the beast took off like a shot. It raced along the shoreline, snorting with anger run wild.

His wife came out of the cottage, crying, "Come back! Come back! Come back!"

Too late, the man realized the truth of the tales of the water-horse. He was stuck fast to the kelpie's sides. Its mane was like writhing snakes, tangling his fingers in a trap. And as the kelpie turned and plunged into the freezing waters, he knew there was no way back.

And so from then on, it was just the woman and her daughter, living alone in the little cottage above the loch.

"We'll starve," said the woman, as the weeks went by. "We cannot till our soil, so what will we do for food?"

"I'll go fishing," said the daughter.

But her mother shook her head. "There's no fish in kelpie waters," she said.

"I can try," replied her daughter. She went down to sit on the rocks and cast out her line. She waited while the sun rose. She waited as it slipped down the sky.

The shores of the loch were deserted, until an old woman appeared.

"Good day," called the girl.

"It is a good day," the old woman replied. "It's the nights I can't stand, when my bones ache with cold."

"Wait here," said the girl, and she ran back to the house and returned with her father's plaid blanket. "Here," she said, handing it over. "We may be poor, but you are poorer still."

"Thank you," the old woman replied. "Take my old shawl in return, and remember these words: it is sometimes better to sit upon a shawl than to wrap it around you."

Then she went on her way. The girl caught one fish that day.

The next morning, she returned to the shores of the loch and there was the old woman again.

"I have no bread," said the woman. "How I'd love a little taste of bread."

The girl opened her bag and took out the last of her bread. "Here," she said.

"Thank you," the old woman replied. "In return, I give you this." And she placed a pouch of salt in the girl's hand. "Now remember my words: salt can be used to calm rather than to cure."

Then she went on her way. That day, the girl caught two fish.

On the third day, the old woman visited the girl by the loch again. This time, she asked for a rope to pull her bucket from the well.

The girl ran to her house and returned with some rope.

"Here is my final gift," the old woman said, and she gave the girl an iron bridle. "Remember my words: iron isn't only used to make a pot."

That day, the girl caught three fish. But she knew that fish alone weren't enough to live on. She thought of her father's plan and the old woman's words, and she waited for the next full moon. Then she picked up the old shawl and the pouch of salt and the iron bridle.

"Don't go!" begged her mother, guessing her

mission. "No one can ride a kelpie and live."

"I have to try," her daughter replied. And so saying, she ran down to the shores of the loch. There stood the kelpie, splashing in the shallows, its coat as black as midnight, tossing its wild mane.

Remembering the old woman's words, the girl threw the shawl over the kelpie and leaped onto its back.

At once the kelpie spoke, in a deep and terrible voice. "No one can ride a kelpie and live," it said.

Then it charged along the shore. Its mane was like writhing snakes, twining her fingers in a trap.

Recalling the old woman's words, the girl threw salt at the mane, and it softened and loosened. But the kelpie just shook its head and began to plunge into the freezing water.

Then the girl remembered the last of the old woman's words and buckled the iron bridle over the kelpie's head.

At once, the kelpie stilled. It became calm and turned tame. The girl rode it out of the water, put it in a harness and set it to work with ease.

The kelpie tilled the field with the strength and speed of ten horses.

"Oh!" cried the mother, as she watched the kelpie at work. "We're saved! We're saved."

When all was done, the girl waited for the next full moon. Then she led the kelpie down to the waters of the loch. She watched it splash for a moment in the silvery shallows, then it plunged into the depths and was gone.

And that is the story of the kelpie of Loch Ness and the only one ever to tame it.

Ivan and the Chestnut Horse

Ivan grew up on a farm on the steppes of Russia, where sun scorched the fields in summer and snow smothered them in winter. It was hard work looking after the farm, and it became even harder after his father died.

Ivan and his two older brothers had promised their father that they would all take care of the farm together. But as soon as the old man was buried, the older boys began to grumble and groan.

"Why leave three of us stuck here?" sighed one. "Surely Ivan can manage on his own."

The other nodded. "Farming is so boring," he said, smoothing his hair. "It suits Ivan; he has no ambition... but you and I deserve more!"

So they left Ivan to do all the work alone, while they spent their inheritance on fancy clothes and fine horses. They rode around the countryside in feathered caps and velvet capes, and thought themselves as good as princes.

Each day, Ivan got up at dawn to milk the cow, feed the chickens and groom the old donkey who pulled the farm cart. Then he would go out into the fields and dig the hard black soil in spring, or cut great armfuls of rustling golden wheat in autumn. He worked until he ached all over, but he never complained or thought of doing anything else, because he had made a promise.

One evening, his brothers came home very excited. A messenger had visited the local town with a royal proclamation. The tsar's daughter, Princess Helena, wished to find a husband. So she had issued a challenge. She would sit in her palace, in the window of the tallest tower, and wait for a horseman brave enough to ride his steed up into the air and kiss her lips at the window.

Each of Ivan's brothers owned a handsome, high-mettled horse, and each thought he would be the one to win the princess.

"Only a horse as bold as mine would dare such a jump," boasted one proudly.

"Ah, but only a prize jumper like mine could leap that high!" bragged the other. He turned to Ivan. "How about little Ivan?" he teased. "Don't you want to try?"

"His poor old donkey couldn't jump a log, never mind leap to the top of a tower!" said the first brother, with a snort.

Ivan said nothing, but continued mending the donkey's harness. He longed to take part, but his brothers were right – he had nothing to ride.

The older brothers spent the next days on horseback, leaping over every fence and hedge on the farm, each determined to prove he was best at jumping. Then they rode off to the town for fancy new riding clothes.

Back at home, they strutted around in front of the mirror admiring themselves. "Fair Helena," they sighed, pouting and trying out kisses on the backs of their hands.

Ivan smothered a laugh and went out to dig the fields. At midday, he sat down on a patch of grass and pulled out a piece of bread for lunch. And as he chewed, he day-dreamed...

He was riding a splendid chestnut horse, its every movement brimming with energy and power. He touched his heels to its sides and away they raced. At his signal, the horse sprang into the air. It soared higher and higher, as if on wings, carrying him up to the window where the princess waited...

"If only..." he sighed ruefully. Then he yawned. Digging was exhausting work and he had woken early.

"Maybe I'll just close my eyes for a minute," he thought. A moment later, he was snoring.

In his sleep, Ivan dreamed his father appeared before him...

"Father!" he cried happily, reaching out...

"Son," said his father, folding Ivan in his arms. "I have come to thank you for all your hard work on the farm. Only you have kept your word! In return, I will tell you how to win the princess.

On the day of the contest, you must go out beyond the fields and call out 'Solnyshko,' which means 'little sun.' A splendid chestnut horse will come to you. He will help you, if you whisper in his left ear and then his right, to tell him what to do."

When Ivan woke, he wondered what to make of it. "I suppose it *was* just a dream," he sighed, rubbing the sleep from his eyes.

"Yet it seemed so real! And really... I've got nothing to lose by trying!"

On the day of the contest, all three brothers got up early. While Ivan milked the cow and fed the farm animals, his brothers groomed their horses until their silky coats shone. Then the brothers saddled up and trotted proudly away.

Ivan watched them go, then set off across the fields. At the edge of the farm, he stopped and called loudly, "Solnyshko!" The sound echoed across the plain... but nothing happened.

Feeling slightly foolish, he was about to go home when he heard a distant drumming. Hoofbeats! The noise grew louder and louder, until suddenly, a magnificent wild stallion thundered into view. Rippling with muscle, his bright chestnut coat shone like burnished copper. And when he neighed, the sound rang out as loud and clear as bells.

Ivan held out his hand and the stallion came closer. Reaching up, Ivan whispered in his ears, first the left and then the right: "Please, will you help me win the fair Helena by jumping up to her window in the tower?"

The stallion dipped his head in answer, as if to say yes. Cautiously, Ivan swung himself up. The wild horse stood calmly and, as Ivan settled himself into the saddle, he felt as bold as any noble or cavalryman.

"Let's go!" he cried, and the chestnut horse raced away. The ground disappeared so fast beneath them, they arrived at the tower only moments after Ivan's brothers. A great crowd of suitors was gathered on horseback about the tower. There were princes on prancing stallions and dukes on dancing mares, generals on hot-blooded cavalry horses and country gentlemen on handsome hunting horses... champion jumpers every one. Everywhere Ivan looked, horses stamped and jingled their bits, and the air smelled of leather and horsehair.

Ivan hung back modestly as the competition began. One at a time, each rider galloped towards the tower, then urged his steed into the air. Each horse obediently gathered itself for a powerful jump, springing bravely upwards… but not one came even close to the window.

High above it all, Princess Helena's eyes roved restlessly over the crowd.

"Is there no one who can meet my challenge?" she sighed. She was a little bored with proud lords and nobles. Then she spotted

Ivan, with his farmer's clothes and honest face. "Who is that?" she asked curiously. The courtiers looked at each other and shrugged.

It was almost the end of the day when Ivan's turn came. He shook the reins and the chestnut horse broke into a canter, covering the ground to the tower swiftly. Just as he reached it, Ivan sat forwards and the horse soared upwards... The crowd gasped. Helena leaned out of her window, her heart aflutter.

Higher and higher flew the horse. It was the best attempt yet. Looking down, Helena saw the top of Ivan's head as he passed beneath her – but that was all. The crowd groaned with disappointment.

As soon as they landed, Ivan twitched the reins and brought the chestnut horse around for a second attempt. With a mighty bound, they soared once more... so close, Helena could

almost touch them – but not close enough for
a kiss.

Ivan did not give up. For the last time, he
turned the horse towards the tower and made
his approach. With thundering hooves, the
chestnut horse devoured the ground. Then,
at Ivan's signal, he leaped into the air,
higher and higher... until Ivan was
on a level with the window and
his lips met those of the princess.
To those watching, it seemed as if
the chestnut horse lingered in the
air while they kissed.

"B-b-but," gasped the courtiers.
"How can that be? It's impossible!"

A moment later, the horse and
Ivan had returned to earth and
galloped away. Princess Helena
leaned out of the tower,

searching for them, but they had vanished.

"Make a decree," Helena told her courtiers. "My heart belongs to that brave horseman, whoever he is. My heart and half my kingdom! Let him return tomorrow to claim his prize."

Far away, beyond the hills, the chestnut horse stopped – and Ivan understood. He jumped down. "Thank you," he whispered.

In reply, the horse shook his mane and whinnied, as if to say goodbye – then galloped off towards the setting sun. Ivan watched him grow smaller and smaller, until he vanished in a glimmer of fiery gold.

The next day, a huge crowd gathered around the tower again – this time, hoping to see the mysterious suitor return. Where was he? *Who* was he? Everyone was gossiping and glancing around, hoping to be the first to spot him.

At the sound of a trumpet, the crowd fell

silent. Then the palace gates creaked open and the princess appeared. Her warm eyes ranged across the waiting faces. She gave not a second glance to the many nobles and dukes, and scarcely paused when she saw two handsome brothers with feathered caps and velvet capes...

Beside them stood a young farmer, on foot now for the chestnut horse had vanished. And when she saw him, she smiled and held out her hands.

"Meet my husband-to-be – your future tsar!" she called out to the hushed crowd. "That is, if you are willing?" she added quickly to Ivan.

Ivan nodded joyfully. "I am," he promised, stepping forwards and putting his hand in hers.

Then the princess led him into the palace, and the crowd cheered so loudly, even the chestnut horse must have heard it, wherever he was. And so they were married, and lived happily for the rest of their days – thanks to the help of Solnyshko, the splendid chestnut horse.

The Magician's Horse

"Birthdays are all the same," complained King Sabur. "Another year, another pile of *boring* presents."

Princess Leyla sighed. "But you must like some of them, Father," she said. "What about the golden fountain of pomegranate juice from the Sultan of Turkey? That was kind of him."

"Boring!" replied the king.

"Or the dozen pure-white camels from the Prince of Morocco?" she tried again. "That was a really generous present, don't you think?"

"Dull, dull, dull," grumbled the king. "I get camels every year. I want something different!"

Princess Leyla sighed. Her father was certainly hard to please. All day, people had come from far and wide to bring extravagant gifts for his birthday. The huge throne room was stacked high with vats of expensive perfume, boxes of priceless jewels and towering displays of sweet-smelling flowers. But the king wasn't grateful at all.

"There's one more person to see you," said Leyla. "He says he's a magician."

"Magician or not," snapped the king. "I bet it'll be another *boring* box of *boring* jewels."

The door to the throne room creaked open. The man who shuffled in was so bent over, the king could hardly see his face. He wore a threadbare cloak and, when he looked up, his face was misshapen, like a reflection in a broken mirror.

The man grunted as he dragged something behind him. It was a large clockwork horse, polished until it gleamed in the sunlight. As he shuffled across the throne room, Princess Leyla admired the excellent craftsmanship. Each delicate metal piece attached snugly to the next to make up the horse's elegant body.

Finally, the shuffling man reached the throne. King Sabur looked at him impatiently.

"What have you brought me?" he demanded. "It can't be just a mechanical toy."

"This is no mere toy, Your Highness," croaked the man. The king and the princess leaned forward, eager to hear what he had to say. "This is *so* much more. Turn the key on the saddle and it will fly!"

The king sat up. He looked more interested than he had all day.

"I don't believe it," he exclaimed loudly. "Let me try."

The king jumped down from his throne and rushed over to the clockwork horse. He slid his foot into a stirrup and heaved himself onto the horse's back.

"Now, work your magic," he said.

Just as he promised, the magician reached up and turned a little golden key on the horse's saddle and...

"Incredible!" the king cried, as the horse's hooves hovered above the

ground. Then off it flew, circling the throne room in graceful arcs. The king whooped in delight, and Princess Leyla clapped and laughed along. She hadn't seen her father this happy in a long time.

When the horse landed again, the king was grinning from ear to ear. He slid off and shook the old man's hand up and down.

"Indeed you *are* a magician," he said. "In return for your gift, I will give you anything you desire. Just name your price."

The magician rubbed his hands together. "I have one request," he said, giggling slyly. "I would like your daughter's hand in marriage."

The king was so enraptured with his new toy, he hardly heard what the old man had said.

"Yes, yes, of course," he said heedlessly. "Now let me try flying again!"

Leyla wasn't laughing now.

"What are you saying?" she said in disbelief. "I don't want to marry that old man. You can't agree to something like that without asking me!"

But it was as if the king couldn't hear her either. He was too busy staring in wonder at his latest present.

"Listen to me, Father," Princess Leyla pleaded. "You're enchanted by that horse."

The magician was coming towards her.

"My new wife..." he said with a nasty leer.

"I refuse to marry you!" cried Princess Leyla, and she ran right past the old man and the king, and jumped onto the horse's back. She turned the golden key and the horse took off again. They flew through the throne room door and straight out of the palace.

Princess Leyla's sudden departure shook the king to his senses.

"What have I done?" he cried. "I didn't listen to my daughter, all for the sake of a shiny new toy."

He ran to the door, but Princess Leyla had already flown so high and so far that the horse was just a dot on the horizon.

"The princess doesn't know how to make the horse come down again," the magician cackled. "I'm afraid she's gone forever. She'll get sizzled by the sun."

The king screamed in rage at his own stupidity and the magician's malice, and threw the magician straight into the dungeon.

Princess Leyla flew through the clouds on the magical horse. She was so angry, she barely noticed how high they were flying.

"I'd rather run away forever than marry that horrible man," she thought.

The horse was flying fast. Below, the princess

saw that she had left her father's kingdom far behind. Rivers looked like narrow ribbons, and lakes scattered the landscape like drops of water.

"Slow down, sweet horse," she called, then told herself not to be so silly. "It's just a toy horse. It can't hear me."

But the horse *did* seem to slow down. Tentatively, Leyla touched its neck, and the horse turned sharply to the right. Then she touched the other side and the horse veered to the left.

But the horse was also flying higher, dangerously close to the sun...

Luckily, Princess Leyla was as sensible as she was beautiful. She wasn't going to get sizzled.

"If something goes up, it must come down," she said to herself firmly. "So if there's a key to make the horse fly, there must be a key to make it come down again."

Being very careful not to lose her balance, she searched for the other key. There it was, inside the horse's left ear – a tiny key that Leyla could only just reach.

She managed to turn it a little and...

"Woooah!" Princess Leyla cried as they hurtled towards the Earth. They were heading straight for a grand building with shining domes of white and gold.

"We're going to hit it!" Leyla yelled, closing her eyes tightly and bracing herself for the crash. But the crash never came. Instead, the horse landed gently on the roof.

"Thank you for bringing me down safely," she whispered. But although she was safe, she had no clue where she was...

"I suppose I'll just have to find out," she said. "I'll be back soon."

Carefully, she crept over the rooftops. Soon she found a small square opening in the stone. It wasn't a window, only a vent to keep the bedroom below cool, but it was big enough for her. She slipped inside.

"Hey!" a voice exclaimed loudly.

Princess Leyla froze. She'd disturbed a young man, who had been sitting on a cushion reading a book.

"Sorry to shout," he said. "I thought you were a burglar. You're not, are you...?"

"No, I'm not!" she replied. "I'm Princess Leyla. Well, I was. I ran away from home, so I'm not sure *who* I am right now."

"It looks like we're both in trouble," said the

young man. "You see, I was kidnapped when I was a boy. I've been locked inside this palace ever since."

"How terrible!" exclaimed Princess Leyla.

"I'm Prince Kristan," the young man explained. "My captor King Cassim conquered my father's kingdom and took me prisoner."

"I can help you escape," said the princess. "Come with me."

Prince Kristan looked nervous. "The palace is full of guards on horseback," he said. "We'll never get past them."

"Don't worry about that," said Princess Leyla, as she climbed back onto the roof, with Prince Kristan following behind. Together they crept across the palace roof.

"So how exactly are you expecting to escape on a *metal* horse?" said Prince Kristan.

"Trust me," said Princess Leyla. She climbed

onto the horse's back and gestured for Prince Kristan to get on behind her. "And make sure you hold on tight."

She turned the golden key and the horse lifted off the ground.

"Wow!" yelled Prince Kristan as Leyla steered them through the air. "Amazing!"

King Cassim was sitting on his balcony, eating grapes and spitting the seeds over the railings. When he spotted the flying horse, he jumped to his feet in horror.

"Intruder!" he spluttered. "Come back here!"

Princess Leyla nudged the horse so it flew right past the balcony.

"We're leaving," called Prince Kristan. "Thanks for nothing."

King Cassim shook with fury. "Guards! Open fire! Destroy that contraption and the wicked witch flying it, too!" he yelled.

Princess Leyla looked down and gulped. The palace grounds were covered in guards on powerful battle horses. They were pointing their crossbows straight at the clockwork horse.

"Watch out!" yelled Prince Kristan as the first arrow whizzed past them, pinging off the horse's metal flank.

The magician's horse flitted through the air, dodging and darting and changing direction at Princess Leyla's lightest touch.

"Help!" cried a guard as Princess Leyla and Prince Kristan swooped past him, just inches from his left ear.

"Hey!" yelled another, as Princess Leyla grabbed his helmet and soared into the sky waving it in the air.

The guards fell into panic. Twenty of the horses bolted in fear, then another twenty, then twenty more...

King Cassim was hopping up and down on his balcony.

"She's a sorceress!" he screamed. "Hold your ground, men. Anyone who runs away will be locked in the dungeon."

But the guards were too frightened to take any notice. They struggled to control their steeds, as the terrified horses galloped away from the strange flying creature.

With no one left to stop them, Princess Leyla and Prince Kristan flew up into the sky and far away, without looking back.

"That was fantastic!" grinned Prince Kristan. "The look on their faces!"

They flew across the bright blue sky. Princess Leyla taught Prince Kristan how to steer the horse and showed him where to find the magical golden keys. Together, they dodged mountains and swooped down waterfalls, skimmed over sparkling lakes and sped through deep valleys.

But later on, as the sun went down, Princess Leyla hesitated. "I don't think we should go any further," she said. "My father's palace is just over there. He promised an old magician my hand in marriage and, well, I'd rather marry someone else."

Prince Kristan squeezed her hand. "It's time for you to go home," he said. "Your father will have realized his mistake, I promise."

Back at the palace, King Sabur was hunched on his throne. Ever since his daughter had flown away on the horse, he had thought of nothing else but his own stupidity and greed. He had given away all his birthday presents to the poor people in the kingdom and vowed never to be so thoughtless again.

"Father?"

A voice shook him from his misery. It sounded like… "Leyla!"

King Sabur rushed from his throne to hug his daughter. After all he had done, she had come back to him.

"I'm so happy you're safe," he sobbed.

Princess Leyla and Prince Kristan lived together in the palace from that day on. Not too long after, they got married and everyone said they were the happiest and kindest couple in the whole kingdom.

And as for the magician? Princess Leyla let him out of the dungeon, but he was never invited to another birthday party again.

Dapplebright

There was once a boy, the youngest of twelve, who inherited nothing from his parents but twelve horses. Eleven of the horses were fine, fully-grown beasts. The twelfth was just a colt, not yet a year old – but he was big for his age, with bold eyes and a bright, dappled coat.

"You're a fine fellow," said the boy, whose name was Hal. He gently ruffled the colt's mane. "But I must sell you if I am to eat."

"Don't sell me," said the colt. "Let me graze in the meadow for another year, and I will grow much bigger and sleeker."

Hal was very surprised, not least to discover the colt could talk. "What an amazing animal," he thought. "Maybe I should take his advice. If I'm wrong, I can always sell him later." So he sold another of his horses, and left the colt in the meadow.

By the next year, the colt was the size of a carthorse, and his dappled coat shone brightly in the sunshine.

"Just look at you," sighed Hal admiringly. "This year, you will fetch a much better price."

"Don't sell me," begged the colt

again. "Let me graze for another year, and I will grow bigger and sleeker still."

Hal hesitated. He needed money, but hated to part with such a creature... and the colt had been right before. "Very well," he agreed, after a moment. So he sold a different horse, and the colt stayed in the meadow, eating and growing, and growing and eating...

By the next summer, he was no longer a colt but a fully grown horse – and what a magnificent beast! He was bigger than any horse Hal had ever seen, and his dappled coat shone as brightly as the sun itself.

"I will call you Dapplebright," said Hal, shading his eyes from the glare. "The king himself has not a horse to compare to you. You will make me rich!"

The horse snorted and shook his head. "Don't sell me! I will help you to make your fortune. Sell the rest of your herd, and use the money to buy me iron shoes and a golden saddle and bridle. You will not regret it!"

Hal nodded slowly. After all, the horse had been right before... and Hal had an adventurous spirit. So he did as Dapplebright asked and bought the very finest horseshoes, saddle and bridle that he could find.

"Very good," said Dapplebright, as he stood in the sunshine in the now-empty meadow, with gleaming shoes and glittering gold trappings.

"Now climb on my back" – he knelt so that Hal could reach – "and let us ride to the king's castle. His daughter has been kidnapped by a troll, but together we can rescue her. Listen carefully and I will tell you exactly what we must do..."

At the castle, the king was very impressed by Dapplebright, but rather less impressed by Hal.

"You're just an ordinary boy!" he exclaimed. "How did you come by such an extraordinary horse? And what on earth makes you think *you* can defeat the troll, where my finest knights have failed?"

"I raised my horse myself," said Hal proudly, looking the king straight in the eye. "And you have nothing to lose by letting me try!"

The king frowned. "Very well," he said slowly. "But you do so at your peril! The troll is powerful and cunning."

"Thank you, sire," said Hal, bowing low. "To help me in my task, I will need certain provisions and a blacksmith for my horse..."

When they left the castle, Dapplebright's feet flashed sparks, for the king's blacksmith had set his shoes with steel spikes. The great horse also carried two gigantic leather saddlebags, packed with everything Hal had asked for: twelve roast oxen, twelve sacks of grain, a huge, heavy metal-plated coat for Dapplebright, and a second golden bridle. No other horse could have carried it all, but Dapplebright loped along easily, as if the bags held nothing but air.

After riding for a day and a night, they reached the troll's mountain. Sheer walls of dark rock rose up before them, as smooth and hard as glass.

"What now?" asked Hal, gazing up.

"We must hope my shoes are sharp enough," answered Dapplebright.

With a sudden burst of speed, he ran straight up the side of the mountain. There was an awful scratching and scraping, as metal spikes met unyielding rock.

Hal felt a sudden surge of hope. Then, with a slithering screech, one hoof slipped, and they crashed back to the bottom.

Again, Dapplebright ran at the mountain. This time, he got halfway before he slipped, bringing down a torrent of rocks and pebbles. But he picked himself up, fixed his eyes on the peak and tried once more.

Rocks and stones flew up into the sky as he galloped furiously, higher and higher – and this time, he made it.

At the top was the troll's cave, the entrance covered by a heavy stone door. Behind it, a voice was singing softly.

"It's her!" cried Hal. He jumped down and called out. "Princess, open the door! We're here to take you home."

"I can't," she answered. "The troll has the only key."

Hal put his shoulder to the door and heaved, but it didn't shift. Then Dapplebright reared up and struck at it with his sharp-shod hooves, again and again, until it cracked apart.

Sudden sunlight flooded into the dark cave, revealing a golden-haired princess. She smiled at Hal with a sweetness that made his heart turn somersaults.

"Quick," said Dapplebright. "We must be off before the troll returns and finds us."

So Hal reached down and the princess reached up, and she scrambled up onto Dapplebright's broad back behind Hal. Then they were away down the mountain,

stones skidding and slipping and sliding all
around them...

Behind them a shout as loud as thunder
boomed across the mountain:

"COME BACK!"

"The troll," groaned the princess.

Dapplebright ran even faster, until
everything around them was a blur.

Back on the mountaintop, the troll roared
in anger and the sky darkened.

"He has sent his wild birds after us," warned
Dapplebright as he ran. "Quick, scatter the corn
from the sacks!"

Hastily, the princess tore open the heavy
sacks and golden corn rushed out.

Fierce and fast, a huge flock of wild
birds came rushing out of the air,
wickedly sharp beaks and claws
ready to attack...

But when the birds saw the corn, they swooped down on it in delight and began to feast greedily, forgetting all about their escaping prey.

The troll roared in fury, and was answered this time with thundering paws and claws...

"He is sending his wild beasts," panted Dapplebright. "Quick, throw down the oxen!"

Hal cast them to the ground just in time. Wolves and wild cats and bears were racing out of the trees, teeth and claws bared. But when they saw the oxen, they stopped and fell upon those instead, tearing huge, hungry mouthfuls.

In the distance, the troll roared one last time, even louder and more fierce than before. This time, to Hal's surprise, Dapplebright stopped dead in his tracks.

"You must do exactly as I say," he warned his

riders. "Climb down and wrap my metal coat around me. Then hide in that bush and don't come out until I tell you. I must face the next challenge alone."

They wrapped Dapplebright in the clinking, chinking coat and hid. They had hardly finished when the ground shook with heavy hoofbeats. Moments later, an enormous horse appeared.

Hal blinked. The horse's dappled coat glowed like the sun. It was the twin of Dapplebright – but where Dapplebright's eyes were wise and gentle, this horse's eyes burned with a deadly flame.

Deep in the bush, Hal and the princess held their breath. The horses circled each other warily. Then the strange horse lunged savagely at Dapplebright, teeth bared.

Again and again, it tried to bite its opponent – but it could not pierce the metal coat.

At last, it began to tire. Dapplebright had been waiting for this moment. He reared up and knocked his foe to the ground, keeping it pinned there with his great weight.

"Now for the golden bridle," he called.

Cautiously, Hal and the princess approached.

As soon as the bridle touched the strange horse, it stopped struggling. Once Hal had buckled the straps, Dapplebright allowed it to stand. All trace of ferocity and fire had vanished from its face. It now stood so meekly, you could have led it with a strand of silk.

The princess ran her hand softly down its neck and it whinnied with happiness. She glanced questioningly at Dapplebright.

"You have nothing to fear," Dapplebright told her. "It was the troll's magic which made her so fierce, but now the spell is broken."

When they set off again, the princess rode on the newly tame horse, with Hal on Dapplebright. Hills sped past in a blur of drumming hooves, until they were back at the castle, where the king greeted them all with delight – especially the princess.

"I'm so happy to have you home safe," he told her, wrapping his arms around her.

Then the king turned to Hal. "I see that I misjudged you," he said. "You alone have defeated the troll and returned my daughter. Now, name your reward."

Hal flushed. "Please, sire, the only reward I desire is a warm stable for our horses and er…" He hesitated, unsure if he dared to go on.

"Speak up," ordered the king kindly.

Hal plucked up all his courage. "And your daughter's hand in marriage – that is, if she will have me?"

"I will," answered the princess at once, blushing with happiness.

They were married the very next week, riding to their wedding on two of the finest horses ever seen.

The White Mare

*O*nce, a king lived with his three beautiful daughters in a magnificent castle. Their mother had died when they were young, leaving behind only treasured memories and a fine white mare named Ghost. The king's youngest daughter, Fifine, was particularly fond of Ghost. She would spend hours grooming the horse's coat until it gleamed like the moon in the night sky.

One afternoon in late summer, Fifine was sitting with her father and sisters in the castle gardens. The two older daughters were discussing how best to find a suitable husband.

"We could hold an archery contest," suggested one, smiling.

"Or a cooking competition!" said the other.

"What do you think, Fifine?" asked the king.

But Fifine wasn't listening. She was watching Ghost graze in the field beside them and wondering if she had time to fit in a ride before dinner.

Suddenly, the king let out a yelp which made Fifine jump. "Ow, I've been bitten!" he cried, scratching the back of his head.

"Hold still, Father," said Fifine. "I can see something moving."

She stood up and plucked a plump flea from behind his ear. The king wrinkled his nose at the sight of it and all three daughters giggled. Only Ghost, the white mare, didn't seem to find it funny. She let out a dreadful whinny.

"Oh Ghost, it's only a flea," said Fifine, holding up the insect for the horse to see.

Then, in front of their eyes, the flea began to grow – as large as a fist and larger still. The king swiftly took it from Fifine, and trapped it in a large barrel. "How strange," he murmured, turning back to his daughters.

Moments later there was a splintering of wood and the enormous flea broke free of the barrel. As it moved threateningly towards them, the king drew his sword and thrust it deep into the flea. There was a long hiss of air and soon all that was left was a large leathery skin.

The astonished king decided to hang the skin in his throne room. "It would take a man of great wisdom to guess what animal this is from," he thought to himself. Then he remembered his daughters' earlier conversation. "That's it!" he cried. "This is just the challenge we need."

The next day, he made an official announcement to the royal court. "The man who is clever enough to name the creature this skin came from can marry one of my daughters!" he declared.

Alas, weeks went by and no one had the faintest idea that a skin so large could come from a tiny flea.

"It looks as if we will have to arrange an archery contest after all," sighed the king.

But before a date had been set for the contest, a stranger arrived at the castle...

Fifine was adjusting Ghost's stirrups in the courtyard when she felt the mare tense up. She followed Ghost's gaze and saw a black stallion

trot in through
the royal gates,
ridden by a
prince all
dressed in gold.
The prince slid
effortlessly from his
horse and asked the

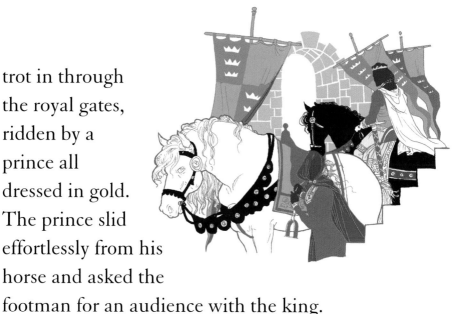

footman for an audience with the king.

"Who can that be?" thought Fifine.

Ghost let out a snort of disapproval.

"I'll find out what he wants," said Fifine.
She gave Ghost a reassuring pat, handed the
mare's reins to the stable boy, then quietly
entered the throne room after the prince.

Fifine watched from the shadows as the
prince first bowed to the king, then looked up at
the wall in amazement.

"Forgive me, Your Majesty," he said politely,

"but… is that a flea's skin?"

The king took note of the prince's golden clothing and his courteous manner. "It is indeed," he remarked, a smile creeping onto his lips. "And your wise observation has just won you the right to marry one of my daughters!"

"Why, thank you!" the prince exclaimed. "Then with your permission I will return tomorrow to choose my bride."

Was it Fifine's imagination, or did he look her way as he turned to leave? She quickly slipped away to tell her sisters the news. They were both extremely excited.

"Was he really dressed in gold?" gasped the middle sister.

"Oh, I hope he picks me," said the elder one, with a sigh.

Only Fifine felt uneasy about the prince, although she couldn't have said why.

That evening she crept down to the stables to talk to Ghost. "I suppose I don't need to worry," she said, idly stroking the mare's silky white mane. "I'm the youngest. The prince isn't going to choose me."

To her utter amazement, for the first time ever, the mare talked back. "He *will* choose you, my child," came her soft, firm voice, "but he is no prince. He's an evil sorcerer who wants to make you his slave. You must listen to my advice and follow it closely."

The princess listened, dumbfounded, as the mare described what she had to do.

To escape the sorcerer's evil clutches, Fifine was to choose Ghost as her wedding present and leave the castle riding on Ghost's back. "Only then do we have a chance of stopping him," whispered the mare.

The next day, while the other two princesses chose their best dresses and carefully curled their ringlets, Fifine tried to look as ugly as possible. In shabby clothes, with her hair uncombed, she hoped the prince would scorn to pick her.

But she hoped in vain.

"Your Majesty, I have made up my mind." The prince was addressing the king, but his eyes were firmly fixed on Fifine. "I choose your youngest daughter."

The king was delighted, the elder sisters were disappointed and Fifine was close to tears.

"My dearest child," said the king proudly. "What a wonderful turn of events. I'm sure this fine prince will bring you every happiness.

Now let me give you a wedding gift from the royal treasury."

"I wish for no treasure, Father," spoke Fifine, a tremble in her voice, "only for Ghost to accompany me on my journey."

The king looked puzzled. "You can't take the white mare," he said.

"Then I won't marry the prince."

A gasp echoed around the throne room and a scowl appeared on the prince's face. Eager to quell the situation, the king quickly consented. "A horse is a strange wedding present, but if it's what you really want..."

"We leave this afternoon," the prince announced abruptly. "We have lots to prepare for our wedding day."

Fifine's wooden trunk was hastily packed and loaded onto the prince's carriage. The prince offered his hand to help Fifine step inside, but she refused. "I'm riding Ghost," she insisted.

Again, the scowl spread across the prince's face, but with a crowd of well-wishers looking on, he couldn't argue. Instead he grabbed her wrist and whispered harshly, "Then you must ride beside me."

The terrified princess did as she was told while they processed through the castle grounds

but, as soon as they were out of the castle gates, Fifine dug in her heels and Ghost reared up.

"Hold on tight!" neighed the mare, breaking into a gallop.

Fifine clung to Ghost's reins as they raced ahead of the prince. She felt the wind through her hair, the drumming of Ghost's hooves and an icy chill in her spine.

"You won't get away from me," yelled the furious prince, spurring on his own black stallion.

Fifine took a fearful look over her shoulder. "He's gaining on us!" she cried.

Her pursuer no longer looked like a golden prince. His eyes were a blazing red, his mouth a twisted scowl. "You're mine!" he snarled.

"Do something, Ghost!" screamed Fifine.

At that moment, the mare skidded to a halt, turned to face the evil sorcerer head on and struck the ground three times with her front hoof. "Open, Earth!" she commanded.

There was a deafening roar as the ground before them ripped apart, creating a deep chasm. The sorcerer and his stallion had no time to react. They plummeted into the cavernous darkness with a ghastly howl that faded to nothing. In an instant, the ground closed up above them.

"You're safe for now," the white mare said softly. "But my magic won't last forever. We should head far away from your family's castle, so the sorcerer can't find you when he returns."

Fifine was lost for words. She lay her head on Ghost's white mane and closed her eyes.

They journeyed for days, until Ghost finally decided they had come far enough. "See that castle in the forest?" said the mare. "A good family lives there. They will look after you."

"Don't leave me!" cried Fifine.

"Reach into my mane," said the mare. "You'll find a little magic flute. Keep it with you at all times and if you ever need me, just play a tune and I shall come."

The next days, months and years were like a beautiful dream for Fifine. She was welcomed into a wonderful family – and fell head-over-heels in love with the eldest son. He was besotted with her too and they were married within a year.

The happy couple were blessed with two boisterous boys, who frolicked in the castle woods, without a care in the world. As time went by, Fifine began to feel as if her encounter with the evil sorcerer had been nothing but a bad dream.

Then one fateful day, her happiness and freedom were threatened once more. Fifine's husband was away hunting and Fifine was in the garden picking apples when she heard her sons cry out. She raced to the woods and found herself face to face with the evil sorcerer. He had an arm around each petrified boy's neck.

"You escaped me last time," he snarled, "but this time I get three souls instead of one."

"You've scared my sons half to death!" cried Fifine. "At least let me calm them with a tune."

"How sweet," mocked the sorcerer, watching with a sneer as Fifine took out her flute and played a few shaky notes.

Instantly, the white mare appeared, more magnificent than ever, her dazzling coat lighting up the shady woodland.

"Ghost!" Fifine cried out in relief.

"You again!" cried the sorcerer, letting the boys go and reaching for his wand.

"Me," said the mare. "And this time my magic is stronger. Open, Earth!" she cried, striking the ground sharply three times with her front hoof.

A vast chasm appeared beneath the sorcerer and he immediately plummeted deep under the ground. In no time, the earth swallowed him and closed up as if nothing had happened.

Fifine held her sons tight while Ghost nuzzled softly into her shoulder.

"You have nothing more to fear," said the mare. "When your husband returns,

take him and your children
to meet your father
and sisters.
They miss you."

"But what about
you?" asked Fifine.

"My job is done," said
Ghost, "and I too must go
home." With that, the white mare
gave a toss of her magical mane, glowed
brighter than the moon... and was gone.

The Seven Foals

There was once a young man named Peter, who journeyed far from home to look for a job. He came across a grand palace surrounded by mountains, with big golden gates in front.

On the gates was a notice:

Stable boy needed. Apply inside.

Peter had never been a stable boy before, but he was determined to get a job. He was reaching for the bell when a sight inside made him stop.

A girl with shining auburn hair was walking through the gardens, wearing a fine gown and a silver tiara.

"She must be a princess..." whispered Peter.

The princess wasn't alone. Around her trotted a group of handsome foals. They held their heads up proudly as they stretched their long, strong legs in the sunshine.

"One, two, three..." Peter counted, but he kept losing track. "Six? No, seven! Seven foals must need a lot of looking after. A stable boy's going to be busy around here."

The princess smiled as she fed them sugar lumps. They even seemed to be listening as she bent down to whisper in their ears.

Peter's heart was doing somersaults. He was

so entranced by the princess, he didn't notice one of the foals trotting over to him.

The foal pushed open the gate with his shoulder. Then he reached through and grabbed Peter's collar with his teeth.

"Woah!" said Peter, losing his footing as the foal pulled him into the palace gardens and brought him face-to-face with the princess.

"Hello," she said. "Who are you?"

Peter thought fast. "Um, ah, I'm here about the job," he gabbled.

"Do you like horses?" she asked.

Peter didn't know anything about horses, but he wanted to please the princess.

"I like yours..." he said.

The princess looked at him closely.

"My foals are very precious to me," she said. "Looking after them is the most important job in the whole palace."

Peter looked around nervously at the seven foals, who were watching him intently with their big eyes. He didn't hesitate for long.

"I'll do it," he told the princess.

"You'll be the fifth stable boy this week," continued the princess. "None of the others were any good. I hope you'll do better."

And with that, the princess walked back to the palace, leaving Peter alone with the foals.

"How hard can it be to keep an eye on some foals?" Peter thought to himself. But before he could even turn around, a foal bolted straight past him, then another, then all seven! They galloped right through the gate and out of the palace gardens, heading up and up, into the snowy mountains.

"Come back!" yelled Peter, but the foals kept galloping, their slender legs a blur as they moved, their dark manes and tails streaming out in the wind behind them.

It was the first minute of his new job as a stable boy and Peter had let the foals run away! He'd have to follow them. He broke into a sprint.

"Woah there! Slow down!" he shouted, but the foals were already far away, their hooves pounding the earth, as they galloped higher and higher into the mountains.

Peter kept running, but he wasn't sure he could keep up much longer. His legs were on fire and his mouth was as dry as straw.

The foals sped past a mountain lake. On the shore, an old woman sat spinning.

"Stop for a drink," she called to Peter as he ran past her.

Peter hesitated. The water looked refreshing and he was so thirsty. But he had to keep going. A stable boy who lost seven horses wasn't going to keep his job for long. "Thanks but I can't stop now," he yelled as he ran past.

"Suit yourself," said the old woman. "All the *other* stable boys stopped for a drink."

The foals were going higher and higher. They didn't stop until they reached another lake, hidden in a dip high up in the mountains. They bent down to drink its cool water.

Peter was startled to see an old woman sat on the shore spinning, just like before.

"Come and sit down by the lake," she said. "You've earned a rest."

Peter was completely exhausted. But what if the foals ran off again? "Thanks, but I can't sit down," he panted. "I'm looking after the princess's foals and I don't want to let them out of my sight for a moment."

The old woman smiled. "You're a determined and trustworthy young man, unlike the others," she said. "I daresay you could break the curse, if you tried..."

"Curse?" Peter asked, intrigued.

"The princess has seven brothers," the old woman continued. "There's a jealous troll who lives further up the mountain. He hated seeing such a happy family. In a fit of rage, he put a curse on the brothers."

"What happened to them?" asked Peter, feeling very sorry for the princess.

The old woman simply pointed to the seven foals. "Can't you see?" she said.

Peter looked at the foals more closely.

He noticed one was taller than the others, with broader

shoulders. Another had a messy forelock that fell into his eyes. Their coats matched the princess's auburn hair exactly.

"The foals are the princess's brothers!" Peter exclaimed. "It's so unfair! Is there any way to turn them back?"

"The foals want to find a young man brave enough to break the curse," the old woman said. "They will take you to the troll's cave. There, you'll find seven enchanted halters. If the foals wear them on your wedding day, the troll's curse will be broken. But you mustn't tell the princess what you're planning."

"I'm brave enough," said Peter. "Wait a second. Did you say *my* wedding day?"

But before the old woman could reply, the foals cantered away again, and Peter ran after them, yelling his thanks to the mysterious old woman as he went. Up and up they ran, until they stopped outside the opening of a cave.

Peter was panting. "What now?" he gasped.

The tallest foal gestured with his elegant head to the cave. It was then that Peter noticed the smell: like dirty dishwater mixed with rotten fish, but even more disgusting.

The foals nudged Peter towards the opening. He approached it cautiously.

From deep inside came a noise like a rumbling avalanche. The troll was asleep – and snoring loudly. Peter held his nose and went in, followed by the foals. He tried to stop his legs from trembling. If the troll woke up, he'd eat them all for dinner.

Inside, the cave was filthy. Peter peered through the darkness. He shuddered in horror at the sight of the troll, his warty greenish skin rising and falling as he slept. He was huge – three times as tall as Peter at least – and heavily built, with fists the size of boulders.

But there was no time to be scared. Peter had a job to do. As his eyes got used to the gloom, he spotted seven halters, just as the old woman had said there would be.

Silently, Peter crept across the cave. The troll grunted in his sleep, but he didn't wake up.

"They're covered in bells," Peter whispered in horror to the foals. "It's a trap. If the bells make a noise, the troll will wake up."

Very gingerly, Peter went to pick up a halter. It was far heavier than he expected, and it nearly slipped out of his hands. The bells jangled loudly.

The troll opened one eye. When he saw the intruders,

he growled with rage and pulled himself to his feet, towering above Peter and the foals.

"Who dares to wake me?" he bellowed.

Peter's stomach clenched in fear. But he thought of the princess and how much she deserved to have her brothers back, and tried to sound brave.

"My name is Peter. I'm here to break the curse," he said stubbornly.

"You'll never succeed," growled the troll. He reached down, grabbed hold of Peter by his left boot and lifted him into the air.

Peter kept as calm as he could, which wasn't that calm at all, given he was being dangled upside-down by a furious troll.

But he needn't have worried: the foals were on his side.

They whirled into action, prancing and dancing around the troll, goading him into a fury. He staggered around the cave, trying to bat them off, and let go of Peter's boot.

Peter flew through the air across the cave and crashed into a wall. His head was spinning, but he picked himself up and rushed over to the halters. He hauled them onto his back and, dodging blows, escaped through the mouth of the cave.

"Come on, boys!" Peter yelled, and the foals raced after him, the troll on their tails.

Peter and the foals fled down the mountain. They ran as fast as they could, but the troll was getting closer and closer by the second.

"We can shake him off!" called Peter, darting from side to side. The foals followed his lead, galloping in zig-zags down the mountainside. The troll tried to catch them, lurching left and right, but he just grabbed at thin air.

Soon they reached the lake where the old

woman sat spinning. By now, the troll's head was spinning too, as he swerved to keep up with the leaping foals. He reached out to grab one, but the foal whipped out of the way just in time. Peter turned to watch in amazement as the troll lost his balance, and toppled over with a deafening crash. He bumped and thumped along the path until... SPLASH! He fell into the lake. He sank straight to the bottom, and was never seen again.

Peter and the foals jumped for joy, and the old woman clapped her hands.

"Now get back and break the curse," she said to Peter and the foals. "Just remember: you can't tell the princess until the wedding day."

Peter and the foals kept running all the way back, until they fell in an exhausted heap in the palace garden.

"You're back!" cried the princess, running to

meet them. "I was so worried, I thought the foals were lost."

"Don't worry, princess," said Peter. "I didn't let them out of my sight for a moment."

"What are those for?" she asked, when she saw the halters.

"I'm afraid I can't tell you just yet," said Peter. "You'll have to trust me."

The princess looked questioningly at him. But, she realized, she *did* trust him. He wasn't like the other stable boys. He hadn't let the foals out of his sight, just as she'd asked, even when they ran off.

Meanwhile, Peter was trying to find the courage to ask a question of his own. He'd already faced a furious troll, but this seemed just as scary...

Peter got down on one knee.

"Will you marry me?" he asked.

The princess glanced at the foals, who nodded their heads encouragingly. Well, if the foals liked this kind and reliable young man, then so did she.

"Yes," she said, taking his hands in hers.

"Let's get married tomorrow!" said Peter. He wanted to break the curse as soon as possible.

"Why so soon?" asked the princess, smiling.

"No time to lose," replied Peter.

The next morning, the princess was putting the final touches to her wedding dress in the royal bedchamber, when she heard a knock at the door.

She opened the door to find Peter standing there, with the seven jangling halters in his arms. Behind him, squished into the palace corridor, were the seven foals.

They poked their heads around the door and impatiently pawed the ground.

"What are you doing in here?" the princess said with a puzzled smile, reaching out to stroke one of the foals on his nose. "The wedding's not for another hour."

Peter didn't answer her. He just grinned and stepped inside. The seven foals squeezed in around him.

"What's going on?" the princess exclaimed. The foals were ruining the carpet.

"Wait and see," said Peter, as he placed the halters onto each foal in turn. The bells made a beautiful sound, like church bells on the day of a wedding.

When the last foal had his halter, something very strange happened. The princess watched in amazement as each foal's soft coat transformed into a soft leather jerkin. Their four legs straightened into the legs and arms of men, while their long noses and teeth shrank to fit seven handsome human faces.

The seven foals had transformed into seven strapping young men.

"My brothers!" cried the princess, hugging each of them in turn. She hardly dared to believe her eyes. After years of heartbreak, she finally had them back – and on her wedding day too!

The eldest brother shook Peter's hand. "You broke the troll's curse," he said. "You are a brave young man – and will make a fine husband for my sister."

"I couldn't have done it without you," replied Peter.

"Now, don't we have a wedding to go to?" asked another of the princess's brothers, whose hair was falling into his eyes.

Peter and the princess got married that day. They had seven best men and, in time, seven sons and a daughter of their own.

The Princess and the Unicorn

Once upon a time there was a proud king who prized beauty above all else. Every item and object in his palace had to be exquisite beyond compare. The palace rooms overflowed with treasures, from golden statues to priceless paintings.

In the gardens there were gilt cages of exotic birds and sparkling pools, filled with fish whose scales flashed like jewels. All who visited would stop and stare.

Every year, the king would desire something new – something even more exciting and exotic. He would send his ministers on near-impossible journeys, deep down into the earth in search of the rarest emeralds, or up into the mountains to find the most delicate flowers.

The king had one child, a daughter. He loved her, but hardly noticed her. His wife, who had died soon after giving birth, had been as beautiful as the treasures in the palace, with hair as gold as summer sunlight, eyes that sparkled blue as sapphires and lips as red as cherries. His daughter, however, possessed none of her mother's beauty. Her hair was neither brown nor fair, but somewhere in between, and her eyes were more like a cloudy sky – but she had a smile that lit up her face like the sun.

The little princess loved her father dearly. She'd bring him the juciest peaches from the palace gardens, look after him when he was sick and her laughter filled the palace. Each day, she longed for her father's attention, but it never came.

Then news arrived...

The king's ministers rushed to his throne room, all jostling to be heard. "A unicorn, sire!" said one. "In the Enchanted Forest," said another. "Pure white with a golden horn," cried a third.

As soon as the king heard the word 'unicorn' he wanted it as he'd never wanted anything before. He rushed to his books on birds and beasts, and gazed at pictures of the magical creature.

"Other kings have treasures and jewels, palaces and castles, the finest horses and the most beautiful brides... but no else has a unicorn. I'll be the envy of every other king. Get it for me!" he commanded.

One by one, his ministers set off to catch the unicorn. One by one, they returned empty-handed. "This task is impossible," they said. "The unicorn starts at the slightest sound and vanishes into the shadows. We cannot catch it."

By now, the king was obsessed. He stayed up late by candlelight, devouring books on

mythical beasts, reading of the unicorn's power and beauty. "I must have it!" he cried.

He sent messengers out into his kingdom, far and wide. "The man who can capture the unicorn can name his prize!"

The hunt was on. Rich men, poor men, knights, farmers, squires and servants all searched the forest for the unicorn. But, as with the ministers before them, they failed.

The king was furious.

Amidst all this, the princess wandered through the palace, feeling more forgotten than ever. One day, she couldn't bear it any more. She sat down by a fireplace and wept.

"Don't cry, little princess," came a voice. The princess looked up to see a strange old woman before her. She had a wizened face and gnarled limbs, and long, white hair that reached down to the floor.

"Who are you?" asked the princess.

"I live in the Enchanted Forest," the old woman replied. "Think of me as your fairy godmother," she added, with a twinkle in her eye. "Now tell me, why have you been crying?"

And so the princess explained about her father and his longing to catch a unicorn, and how he seemed to notice her less and less.

The old woman tutted and nodded. At last she said, "What your father needs is a lesson. Leave it with me. And however bad things may appear, do not despair."

"Thank you," said the princess. She wiped away her tears and followed the old woman to the throne room where the king sat.

"I can bring you the unicorn, Your Majesty," the old woman declared. "I can succeed where others have failed. But you must give me something in return."

"Whatever you wish," said the king. "Name your price."

"I want your daughter," replied the old woman. "I'll return a year to the day and take her away."

"Oh!" cried the princess, in shock and surprise.

But the king brushed her aside. All he could think of was the unicorn. "Done," he said.

"Then come with me, Your Majesty," said the old woman.

She led the king to the forest's edge, where she handed him a silver cord, fashioned into a halter. "Follow this path to the heart of the forest," she said, "until you come to the Silver Pool. There, by the light of the moon, you'll see the unicorn. Throw the halter over its head and it will be yours."

The king did as he was told. As softly as he

could, he walked the forest paths, until he came to the Silver Pool. And there, drinking from its waters, was the unicorn, shining by the light of the moon. Its horn gleamed gold, and its coat was as pure as snow. The king raised his arm and threw the halter around its neck. He had snared his prize.

The king led the unicorn home and kept it in his palace, in a gilded cage. "I'll be the envy of every ruler in the world. It's perfect," he murmured.

The princess loved the unicorn too. Every day she came to feed him and stroke his velvet coat through the bars of the cage. He seemed to carry with him the secrets of the forest, of silent pools and moonlit skies. Looking at him, she began to wonder what the world might be like beyond the palace walls.

"We're the same, you and I," she would say. "Both trapped in this palace."

And the unicorn would bend his head and place his soft muzzle in the palm of her hand, as if in sympathy.

The months passed, and all the while, the princess's heart was breaking, that her father had agreed to send her away. She remembered the old woman's words, that she shouldn't despair, but her hope that her father would change his mind was fading fast.

Then one moonlit night, when the princess sat up with the unicorn, she said, "Why should I wait to be sent away?" She looked at the unicorn... "I wish we could both escape."

As the unicorn's wise black eyes met hers, she felt courage grow in her heart. "I can do this," she whispered to herself. "I can be brave."

She ran to her father's chest, where she knew he kept the key to the golden cage. Then she returned and, taking a deep breath, unlocked the door.

The unicorn whinnied gently and bent his head, as if in invitation. The princess hesitated only a moment, then swung herself onto his back. This time the unicorn tossed his head and whinnied long and loud. Then he cantered out of the palace, his hooves clattering across the floor, a gleam in his starlight eyes.

They galloped through the palace door and across the lush green lawns.

The king saw them from his window. "Come back!" he bellowed. He sent out his army after them, but the unicorn was as swift as the wind.

As dawn broke, his men returned alone. Both the unicorn and the princess were gone.

And now, too late, the king realized how much he missed his daughter – her smiles and her laughter, her presence in the palace, her loving warmth compared to his cold, bright treasures.

The king sent his ministers to search for the princess far and wide. He no longer cared for his sparkling jewels or his dazzling birds. All he wanted was his daughter's return.

At the year's end, came the old woman, just as she had promised.

"I've come to claim my prize," she said. "Where is your daughter?"

The king shook his head. "She's gone," was all he could answer.

Then you must give me something else," the old woman replied.

"Take my treasures!" cried the king sadly. "Take everything. I don't care. None of it is worth as much as my daughter's love. That, it turns out, is the greatest treasure of all."

"Do you really mean it?" the old woman asked quietly.

The king nodded and the old woman looked deep into his eyes. "I believe you," she said.

She clicked her fingers, and across the lush green grass came the unicorn. And on his back was the princess, smiling her beautiful smile.

The king opened his arms and his daughter flew into them. "At last," said the king. "I thought I would never see you again. I'm sorry I never noticed you. I'm sorry I never loved you as I should."

In reply, the princess smiled and hugged her father tighter still.

"But I don't understand," said the king. "Where have you been?"

"She's been with me in the Enchanted Forest," the old woman replied. "We thought it might be good for you to be without your daughter for a while. So Your Majesty, let's see... which would you rather keep – your daughter or the unicorn?"

"My daughter," replied the king, without a moment's doubt.

"Then my job is done," said the old woman, with a smile. "Or nearly..." she added, turning to the princess. "As your fairy godmother, I have yet to grant you a wish."

"A wish for me?" gasped the princess. "But I have everything I want..." Then her eyes alighted on the unicorn, standing tall and proud

on the palace lawn. "Well, *nearly* everything," she thought. And she bent down to whisper in the old woman's ear.

"A good wish," the fairy godmother replied. "You have chosen well, my dear."

"Did you wish for more treasures?" asked the king. "For rubies, sapphires, emeralds? Great chests of gold? For let me tell you, none of these will bring you happiness."

"You'll just have to wait and see," the princess replied, smiling.

From that day on, the king and his daughter lived happily together in the palace. And once a month, when the moon was full, the unicorn would return, to take the princess on magical moonlit rides – just as she had wished.

The Good-Luck Horse

In a remote valley in China, a farmer named Jun lived on a small farm, with his son, Jin. They were not rich, but they did own one horse named Jet. She was sleek and beautiful, with a glossy black coat and a long, silky mane. Not only that, but she was strong and faithful. Her strength made tilling the fields much easier.

All their friends thought they were lucky to have such a fine horse.

One bright, sunny morning, Jun woke up early as usual, and went out to feed Jet. To his surprise, her stall was empty. He checked the yard and then the fields. She wasn't there. Together with Jin, he searched all around the village, along the river and in the woods.

There was no sign of Jet anywhere.

"She must have escaped into the mountains," said Jun. "The land is so rugged and wild there, we will have no chance of finding her now."

When the people in the nearest village heard that Jun and Jin had lost their horse, they came to offer their sympathy. They were fond of Jun and knew how much he treasured Jet. They wondered how he and Jin would cope without her. "What bad luck to lose such a precious horse," they told him.

You can imagine their surprise when Jun did not seem upset at all.

"It could be good luck. It could be bad luck. Who knows?" was all he would say.

"How could losing your only horse possibly be good luck?" his friends remarked to each other in astonishment.

Jun and Jin did their best to look after the farm without Jet, but it was a struggle.

A few months later, Jun was digging the fields when he spotted something gleaming black in the distance, right up in the mountains. Curious, he kept watching...

His heart gave a leap of joy as the familiar outline of his beloved horse came into focus, galloping in his direction. Just behind her, he could make out more horses, a whole herd of them. These horses looked very different – smaller, with thick, light brown coats, short dark manes and strong, sturdy legs. Jun knew they must be wild horses from the mountains. They followed Jet all the way to the farm.

Jun and Jin were thrilled to see Jet again. They welcomed the wild horses onto the farm too, giving them oats to eat and making them a bed of fresh straw in the barn. Wild horses were rarely seen in the valley, so their curious friends flocked to have a look, and congratulate Jun and Jin on their good fortune.

"If you can tame these horses, you will be able to work even more of your land and become rich. We are so happy for you," they said. "You deserve this good luck."

They were puzzled when Jun did not seem as excited as they were.

"It could be good luck. It could be bad luck. Who knows?" he spoke calmly.

Jun and Jin set to work taming the wild horses, slowly gaining their trust. Eventually, one horse seemed ready to ride. Very gently, Jin put a bridle onto him and led him into the field.

Jin was only young, but he was a skilled rider. Usually, he could coax any horse to do what he wanted. But as soon as he mounted, the horse started bucking and rearing, trying to throw him off.

Jin held on tight, but the horse was too powerful. Jin was flung to the ground with a thud, leaving him in agony, as the horse galloped off. Jun rushed over as fast as he could, and found his poor son lying there, his legs broken.

For months, Jin could not leave his bed. The doctor said it would be a long time before he would be able to walk again, and even longer before he could ride. "And he will always have a limp," he warned.

There was no way Jun could look after a whole herd of wild horses on his own, so he opened the farm gate and let them out, for them to find their way back to the mountains.

Jin was heartbroken. Jet was the only thing that kept his spirits up, as he watched her from his bedroom window, dreaming of cantering across the fields.

People in the village were very kind and did their best to cheer him up. They visited daily, bringing food and homemade remedies. They also tried to console Jun on his terrible luck.

"Those wild horses Jet brought down from the mountains did not turn out to be so lucky after all," they sighed, shaking their heads.

"It could be good luck. It could be bad luck. Who knows?" was Jun's only reply.

His response was now familiar to the villagers – and they had seen how good luck could lead to bad luck, and how bad luck could turn out to be good. Yet this time, with Jin lying in bed with broken legs, it seemed impossible to think of his accident as good luck.

While Jin was recovering, a military official came around all the houses in the area to announce that a war had broken out with the next province. Every fit and healthy young man had to go and fight. The troops gathered and off they marched. All except Jin.

Jin felt useless trapped in bed while his friends were being brave on the battlefield. Then, reports started to come back that things were not going well. The fighting was brutal and there were many injuries. Eventually, news arrived that not one man from their area had survived.

As the villagers gathered to mourn those who had died, people came up to Jun and told him, "If Jin had gone to fight, he would almost certainly have been killed too. You are lucky your son is still alive."

Jun felt truly sorry for the friends who had lost their sons. Of course, he was relieved that Jin was alive, and that they had Jet back on the farm to help them.

Jun's friends could never have believed he would turn out to be the lucky one, when poor Jin broke his legs. But now they knew he was right when he said, "It could be good luck, it could be bad luck. Who knows?"

The First Horses

$\mathcal{P}$oseidon, God of the Seas, was in love
– not with a sea-goddess, but with
Demeter, Goddess of the Harvest, with
hair the rich gold of ripened corn, ringed
by a golden crown.

Demeter was searching the far corners
of the Earth for her daughter, Persephone,
but she was nowhere to be found.

"Never mind about your daughter," said Poseidon. "Come with me and rule the seas."

Demeter only shook her head. "All I want is my daughter back," she told him. "I have no time for love."

"Set me a task," insisted Poseidon, "as a test of my love. Then I can prove myself to you."

Demeter only looked at him scornfully, but to be rid of him she replied, "Make me a beautiful creature – the most beautiful the world has ever seen. Only then will I return your love."

So Poseidon returned to his ocean kingdom and set to work. He stirred up the waters of the deep with his three-pronged trident and breathed life into the cold, dark waves.

A fish formed out of the waters, sleek and fluid and fast. It was stormy blue with a lashing tail and a fin to cut through the waves.

It flashed through the water then leaped into the air, like an arrow sent up from the deep. Poseidon watched it proudly. "This creature," he thought, "is sure to win Demeter's love. It's as bold and strong as the sea itself. It is beautiful to behold."

Then he rose up from the deep and called Demeter to the clifftops, so that she might come and admire this gesture of devotion.

"Watch!" he commanded. "See what I have created, just for you."

Demeter watched the creature as it danced in and out of the waves. "A creature of the sea!" she cried. "This is pure vanity – a plaything of your ocean world that can never belong on land. It is too cold for my idea of beauty. You won't win my love with this."

In fury, Poseidon struck the waters with his trident, lashing up mountainous waves. "Not good enough?" he roared. But he found he was raging at her retreating back.

"Still, I will impress her," he vowed. "I'll make another creature. It will be bold and strong like the sea, but this time, it will breathe air. I'll give it a mane of hair as soft as Demeter's. I'll make it white like the crest of the waves. It will be a symbol of our love."

Poseidon stirred the surface of the sea with his trident, until it frothed and bubbled and foamed, then he blew through the spray until a creature appeared. It had a fish's tail, with gleaming scales, and two strong legs with hooves that flashed bronze in the sun. Poseidon created four of them and sent them to play in the waves.

"Demeter!" he called across the clifftops. "This time I have triumphed. Behold the hippocampi! They are made from the foam of the sea, but they breathe the air above the waves. Have I not proved my love to you now?"

Again, Demeter looked scornful. "Hippocampi?" she scoffed. "Beautiful? Look at their fishy tails. What use are they to me on land? You have still not won my love."

By now, Poseidon's fury was mounting like an ocean storm. How dare Demeter refuse him twice? He would try once more – and this time, he would create a creature so beautiful she would never be able to deny him. He set to work, his trident combining clouds and sea and sky, and when he was finished, he knew that here was a gift worthy of the highest love.

"Demeter!" he called, and when she came he bid her stand upon a sandy beach. He smiled broadly, sensing victory.

"You wanted the most beautiful creature the world has ever seen? I have created it."

Poseidon raised his trident and with all his might he drew back the sea so it rose, up, up, up into a towering wall of water. Lined along its crest, rising from the foam, were white horses, pawing, snorting, tossing their silken manes. Then, at Poseidon's command, they began riding down the waves.

Demeter watched in wonder as their hooves pounded through the water – until they emerged, glistening, galloping onto the sands. She saw their silken manes and streaming tails and the strength in their four-limbed stride. She reached out to touch them as they passed her by, and their skin was warm and soft.

"The most beautiful creature in the world," said Demeter. And she looked at Poseidon, and this time he saw love in her eyes.

Poseidon reached out his hand to her. Then he hestitated – and took it back. His wounded pride had turned to anger. "Can I really love you," he wondered aloud, "after you've put me to such a test? No... I cannot. I am Poseidon, brother of Zeus and Hades, Earthshaker and God of the Seas. I bow to no one. Twice you rejected my gifts," he went on. "Twice you scorned my offer of love. Now, I take it back."

And on those words, he plunged back down to the ocean depths.

As for Demeter, she was not left broken-hearted. She had heard news of her daughter, deep in the underworld. For six months of each year, she was told, her daughter would live there. But for the other six months, her daughter would be restored to her.

So the love story of Demeter and Poseidon was never to be. But from that spark of desire, Poseidon created the first horses, and from them came all the rest – the four immortal horses of the Sun God; winged horses to battle monsters; gold-bridled horses to drive the gods' chariots through the space between the earth and the heavens. There were horses for men to ride on, too, horses to till the fields and pull the carts.

And, last but not least, there were the horses of the sea. For after spurning Demeter, Poseidon caught the hippocampi and harnessed them to his chariot. Then, with a crack of his golden whip, he would drive them, proud and mighty, across the ocean waves. From time to time sailors would see him, rolling across the waters, pulled on by his fishtailed, storm-footed steeds.

The Horse, the Fox and the Lion

"You've served me well," said the farmer to his faithful old carthorse. "But now you're too old to pull my cart and I can't keep an animal who doesn't work. I'm sorry but you must go and find somewhere else to live."

The horse looked at the farmer sadly. It was true, he was old and worn out, but he didn't want to leave the farm where he had spent so many happy years.

The farmer had made up his mind.

"I can't keep you here," he said firmly, opening the gate and sending the horse on his way with a slap. "Don't come back unless you're as strong as a lion again."

The horse took one last look at his old home, and set off. After the hustle and bustle of the farmyard, he felt very alone.

Soon, he reached a forest. "I'm just a useless carthorse," he said out loud to the trees. "It's no wonder the farmer doesn't want me anymore."

A fox was having his breakfast nearby. He pricked up his furry ears at the sound of the

horse's heavy hooves and sad voice.

"What's up, my friend?" he cried, jumping out of his den and into the path of the horse. "It's a beautiful morning and I don't like to see any creature unhappy."

The horse took one look at the sprightly fox and sighed heavily.

"I'm too old," he said, gloomily. "The farmer won't keep me unless I work."

"Oh dear, my dear fellow!" chattered the fox. "Surely we can do something about this."

"What *can* we do?" said the horse. "The farmer said I can't come back unless I'm as strong as a lion again, and that's never going to happen."

The fox thought for a moment. Then he grinned. He could think of a way of helping the old horse – and making a little mischief too.

"Don't worry," he said. "I have a plan!"

"I'm too tired for plans," moaned the horse.

"Not this one!" said the fox. "Follow me."

The fox bounded off through the trees with the big old carthorse stomping reluctantly behind him. What good was a plan? He wasn't going to get any younger. Still, he had nothing to lose...

"We're almost there," called the fox from up ahead. "Keep up!"

They reached a clearing in the forest. "For our plan to work, you will need to do three things," said the fox sagely.

"Oh dear," sighed the horse. "They're not too energetic, are they?"

"Lie down. Close your eyes. Stay still," commanded the fox. Well, the horse could do *those* quite easily. He lay down in the middle of the clearing and kept as still as he could, squeezing his eyes tightly shut.

The fox bounded off again, his nose to the ground. Sniffing, he tracked a trail, all the way to... the lion's lair.

"Yoo-hoo, dear lion!" he called.

"What do you want, Fox?" she growled. Crossly, she crawled out of her lair.

"I just wanted to tell you," said the fox casually, "that there's a huge meal lying in the forest. I thought you should be the first to know about it."

The greedy lion licked her lips. "A meal, you say?" Her tummy rumbled loudly at the thought of food.

"A feast!" said the fox. "Follow me and I'll show you the way."

The fox led the lion to the clearing. The lion saw the horse lying perfectly still, and started drooling. An animal that big could keep her going for days.

"Wait a moment," said the fox slyly. "Wouldn't it be awful if any of the other animals in the forest found out about this tasty treat? Why not take your dinner back to your lair to enjoy in peace?"

That sounded like a brilliant idea to the lion. She didn't like sharing her food.

"Let me help you," said the fox. "If you tie the horse's tail to your own, it'll be far easier to drag him back."

The lion hesitated a moment – then turned around and held out her tail. "What a helpful fox," she thought to herself.

So the fox tied the lion's tufted yellow tail to the horse's long white one. "I'll make sure the knots are nice and tight," he said.

And all the while, the horse stayed perfectly still, until...

"GIDDYUP!" cried the fox. Up the horse jumped and the lion was thrown to the ground, her paws flailing in the air. Despite his age, the carthorse still towered over the lion.

"Pull!" called the fox, springing onto the horse's back.

The horse stomped back towards to the farm, the lion bumping and thumping along the forest floor behind him. "This is a rotten trick," she growled.

When they reached the farm, the farmer rushed out of the farmhouse at the familiar sound of hooves.

His mouth fell open when he saw the three animals now in the farmyard. The old carthorse was back! On his back sat a fox with a big grin on its face. And there, tied to his tail, was a real growling, yowling lion!

For a few moments, the farmer was speechless with surprise.

The horse pawed the ground nervously. What would the farmer think of him, bringing a fox into the farmyard, never mind a hungry lion! Would he be angry at such a trick?

But then the farmer threw back his head and started laughing. He gasped and guffawed until tears streamed down his face.

"What a fantastic joke!" he gasped, when he finally caught his breath. "I said you'd need to

be stronger than a lion, and here you are –
you've brought me a lion!"

The fox winked at the horse. His plan had
worked out perfectly.

The farmer approached the lion gingerly.
Pathetically, she batted the air with her paws.

"If I untie you, do you promise to go back to
the forest?" the farmer said. The lion – who
had had quite enough of being tied up like a
turkey – nodded.

The farmer untied the lion's tail and she
went slinking back to her lair, very embarrassed
at falling for such a trick.

"You've given me the best laugh I've had in
ages," said the farmer, patting his old horse
fondly. "And I'm a man of my word. You are
clearly as strong as a lion, so you're welcome to
live here as long as you want."

He led the horse to the stable, covered in

fresh straw. The horse settled down happily. He was back home at last, and for good this time.

And the fox? He bounced back into the forest looking for some other trick to play. Sometimes it's worth causing a little mischief.

Pegasus

$\mathscr{P}$egasus, white-coated with soft, feathered wings, was the stallion of the gods. Sometimes he would soar through the skies, carrying thunderbolts for Zeus, king of the gods. But he was also the horse of the Muses – nine goddesses who reigned over music, poetry and art.

With a strike of his hoof on Mount Helicon, the home of the Muses, Pegasus had opened up a divine spring. Poets drank from it for inspiration. They would also call upon him for help with their art, and Pegasus would rush to their service. Until the day a starving poet decided to use him not for art, but for money...

"Words won't buy me food to eat," the desperate poet declared. "I've had enough of writing and rhyming. I'll sell this horse to the highest bidder, whoever he may be." And he bridled Pegasus and dragged him along to the nearest market.

As they entered, Pegasus pawed the ground nervously, sensing something was wrong. The stalls were packed with sheep and goats for sale. The hot air buzzed with angry flies and everyone turned and stared at the huge white horse. He was like nothing they had ever seen before. Full of pride and anger, Pegasus reared up, beating his wide wings, scattering the onlookers. Then he plunged forwards, trying to make his escape, but the poet held on tight, and a crowd of people blocked his way.

"He's too wild to be tamed," said one. "Look at the size of him!"

"Yes," agreed another. "I don't like the look of those wings. I'd not have him for my horse."

"You'll have to sell him cheap," jeered a third, loudly.

At the back of the crowd, a farmer heard and came forward.

"I'm looking for a cheap horse," he said. But when he saw those wide, beating wings, he too stepped back. "Hmm," he said. "I could crop them, I suppose."

"Or tie them down?" suggested the poet, desperate to make a sale.

"Yes," agreed the farmer, nodding, "I'll have him. I'll give you twenty silver coins for him."

"Agreed!" cried the poet, delighted at the deal. He didn't even try to make a better bargain. He'd been worried for a moment that he wouldn't get anything at all for such a strange-looking creature. And so, for twenty silver coins, he sold the proud winged stallion as a simple farmhorse.

With a tug of the bridle, the farmer pulled Pegasus out of the jostling market and began the journey home to his clifftop farm.

"You've got strength," said the farmer,

chatting half to Pegasus, half to himself, "I can see that. Maybe I will try you pulling one of my carts."

Finally, in the late afternoon, they reached the farm. The farmer didn't allow Pegasus to rest. He was too eager to test the strength of his new horse. He tied down Pegasus's wings with thick, strong rope and then hung saddlebags over the horse's broad back, before loading them up with figs and oranges.

"I need to take these to the villagers in the valley," he said. "Let's see how swiftly you can carry them down. Careful now. I don't want them bruised." Then, with a swish of his whip, he called out, "Move on!"

Pegasus turned his head and looked at the farmer out of his shining black eyes. Then he reared up, bucking and rearing to shake off the heavy load.

"Whoah there!" called the farmer. "Steady! Steady! Don't get ideas above your station."

But this only seemed to enrage Pegasus more. He pounded his hooves, more used to cutting through the air then carrying sackloads of fruit. Then he reared up once more and this time he was off, galloping down the track. The saddlebags bumped against his sides. Figs and oranges flew out in all directions, before raining back down onto the dusty soil.

"Come back," cried the farmer, racing after him. "I command you to STOP!"

By now, Pegasus had reached the end of the path, where the cliff dropped away to the valley below.

Pegasus stopped, just as the farmer had commanded,

and he waited. The farmer came closer.

"You stay right there," he ordered.

Pegasus whinnied.

The farmer came a step closer still. "I'll teach you how to behave."

Pegasus pawed the ground.

"I'll show you who's master now."

At that, Pegasus bowed his head and bucked with all his strength, throwing the saddlebags, fruit and all, tumbling over the cliff edge. Then he meekly trotted all the way back to the farm.

That night, the farmer discussed the matter with his wife.

"Why don't you try him with the cart tomorrow?" she suggested. "You have passengers to take to town. He could pull it by himself – he looks strong enough to take the place of two horses."

So the next morning, Pegasus was tied to the

cart alone, instead of the usual pair of horses. The passengers muttered suspiciously about the winged horse, but the farmer reassured them all would be well.

At first he was right. Pegasus went fast and without a fight. But then his eyes turned skywards and his wings strained at the ropes that bound them, as if longing for the freedom to soar through the skies. His hooves pounded faster and faster over the ground.

The people cried out in fear. "Stop!" they yelled. "Slow down." But nothing would still his speed.

Pegasus raced across fields and marshes, over moors and grassy plains. The farmer called out to him and pulled with all his might on the reins, but he couldn't hold Pegasus back. At last, with the cart smashed nearly to pieces, Pegasus came to rest on a mountaintop.

The furious passengers spilled out of the cart to begin the long walk home. As for the farmer, he was determined to break this horse – whatever it took – and to bend him to his will.

"I'll work him so hard, he'll never dare rear up again," he declared furiously. "I'll give him so little to eat, he won't have the strength for tricks like this."

From then on, Pegasus was forced to till the fields with a heavy, lumbering ox at his side. Day after day he worked the soil, on little food and no rest, until he was so weak his legs trembled and his mane hung lank against his scraggy coat.

Then one day, feeling the last of his spirit sap away, Pegasus tumbled to the ground and lay, quiet and still, on the dusty ground.

The farmer was beside him in an instant, swiping down at him with a whip.

"Get up!" he cried. "How dare that poet sell me such a worthless beast."

"Worthless?" said a voice behind him, and the farmer turned to see a golden-haired youth. He carried a lute in one hand and a golden band encircled his head.

"Who are you?" demanded the farmer.

"A poet and a musician," the boy replied. "I've heard tales of a white, winged horse who can inspire poetry and soar through the skies."

"Well he's no good to me," the farmer replied. "He can't even pull a cart, let alone till the fields."

"I think I could show you what he can do," said the boy. "May I try?"

"Ha!" laughed the farmer. "It'll be a miracle if you can get him to rise from the dirt."

Without another word, the boy stepped over to where Pegasus lay and whispered in his ear. Then he lifted away the harness. Unshackled, Pegasus rose from the ground on shaking legs. Next, the boy untied his wings and Pegasus stretched them out, his feathers ruffling in the breeze. The boy tucked his lute under his arm and climbed onto Pegasus's back.

"Oh I wouldn't do that," said the farmer. "He's not to be trusted, you know."

"I'm not afraid," said the boy, smiling.

Sensing freedom, Pegasus began to beat his wings. His eyes sparked and god-like, he rose into the skies. The farmer watched, amazed, as the beast that had lain in the dirt flew up and up, until he was no

more than a white speck among the clouds.

"Hey!" called the farmer. "Come back here! If he can do that, I might get some work out of him yet."

But nothing would persuade Pegasus and his rescuer to return. The winged horse flew on into the airy blue, swooping and diving, his hooves glinting gold in the sun. The boy on his back cried out for joy as together they flew through the heavens, finally coming to rest on Mount Helicon. There the Muses sat beneath the shade of an olive tree, patiently waiting.

"So, Pegasus," they said. "We sent a poet to save you. We're sorry he took so long to find you, but at last you have returned home."

Pegasus shook his proud mane and stamped his hooves, happy to be back where he belonged.

The Old Horse of Atri

Perched halfway up a mountainside in Italy, sat the sleepy town of Atri. It was a pretty little town, surrounded by fields where horses grazed, but it was very quiet and nothing much ever happened there.

Then, one day, a huge silver bell appeared at the top of the tower in the market square, with a long rope hanging to the ground beside it. The bell shone brightly in the sunlight... but why it was there was a mystery.

A curious crowd had soon gathered around it. Each person had their own theory about this new addition to the town.

Suddenly, a loud trumpet bellowed and the local lord rode into the square, followed by a long procession of attendants. The crowd hushed and waited eagerly to hear what he had to say.

"This is the Bell of Justice," the lord declared. "It is for everyone in Atri, from the tallest man to the smallest child. If anyone is wronged, pull the rope to ring the bell and justice will be done."

This idea was greeted with great enthusiasm

by the crowd. Most of the time, there was
very little amiss in Atri, but from that day on,
if someone felt wronged, they rang the bell.

"*Ding ding, ding ding!*" chimed the bell, and
the judge would hurry to the square and put
the matter right.

Over many years, the threads of the rope
slowly unravelled and broke off. The rope
became shorter and shorter until only the tallest
man in the town could reach it.

"Something must be done," declared the
lord, when he noticed that the bell was no
longer of use to everyone in Atri. "But who
can find a rope long enough to replace the
old one?"

Rope that long was not easy to find in such
a small town, but one man was struck with
inspiration. A glorious vine grew up the side of
his house. It wound its way up onto the roof

and right along the eaves. He ran home and gently tugged the vine until it came tumbling down. He bundled it into a basket and carried it back to the square. Everyone agreed it was long enough to make an excellent replacement, until a rope could be found.

The vine was tied to the bell. It hung right down to the ground, with its leaves and tendrils still hanging off it. Now even the smallest child in the town could ring the bell, and life in Atri went on as happily as it had before.

Not everyone in Atri was quite so content. At the edge of town, an old knight lived all on his own. In his youth, he had won many brave victories on the battlefield, and had kept many horses and hunting dogs. But now, he had grown tired of hunting and shooting. Grooming the horses, feeding them and cleaning the stables was hard work. He would rather stay inside and count up his money.

"What use are all these animals to me?" he moaned to himself. "They are not going to keep me comfortable in my old age. They will have to go."

So he sold his animals one by one, greedily stacking up the piles of gold they made him.

When he came to his last horse, he hesitated for a moment. This horse had carried him faithfully on the battlefield and together they had been on many adventures.

"I feed you and groom you, but what do you do for me now?" the knight thought.

Then he remembered how impressive the horse made him look on festival days, when they paraded through the town together.

What a sight they looked, the knight with his gleaming outfit, riding high above the crowds on the back of his magnificent charger.

The old knight puffed up with pride at the thought.

"All right, I'll keep you. But don't think I'll be buying you any more of those expensive oats and barley. There's some grass in the field. You can graze out there."

The knight was true to his word and turned the horse out into the field. The horse managed to find a few tufts of grass to nibble, but most of it was burned by the sun. This once beautiful creature grew thin, ragged and sad.

"What a useless excuse for an animal you are!" said the knight, one rare day when he bothered to go outside. "I'd be ashamed to be seen riding you now. I don't even think you'd fetch much cash. There's only one thing left to do. Go on, get away now, shoo!"

The knight opened the field gate and chased the poor animal out into the lane. "You're on your own now!"

The horse was hungry, so took his chance to hunt for fresh food. He spotted a few scraps of hay, which had fallen off a hay wagon. He gobbled them up and followed the lane hoping to find more. It was midday and the streets of the town were silent. Everybody was at home, dozing, keeping out of the sun.

At last, the horse spied the juicy green vine hanging from the bell tower. It looked delicious! He wasted no time. *Munch, munch, crunch*

– he hardly stopped for breath. Tugging at the vine, he reached higher and higher for more.

"*Ding ding, ding ding!*" came the clear chime, breaking the silence.

The people of Atri groaned. Who could possibly need justice during their pleasant, midday snooze? The judge rolled over in his bed and sleepily opened his eyes. Realizing what he heard, he leaped out of bed, put on his robes and hurried to the square.

There was no one in sight, only a solitary horse! People began to gather, burning with curiosity. As they watched, the horse took another bite of vine, ringing the bell again.

"The horse wants justice!" they cried.

"That is the old knight's horse," said one woman. "He used to be so beautiful, but look at him now, all skin and bone. The knight is too busy counting his money to look after him."

"Justice must be done!" everyone shouted.

"Very well then," said the judge. "Bring the knight to me."

Reluctantly, the old knight appeared before the judge.

"This horse has served you well over the years," the judge said solemnly. "He has carried you on the battlefield and in our town processions, but in return you have treated him terribly."

The knight looked embarrassed – and worse was to come.

"As a punishment," continued the judge, "you must give half your gold to build a new stable and buy him all the food he needs. We, the people of Atri, will look after him from now on."

Spending any of his precious money was hard for the knight, but half his gold? It was almost more than he could bear – yet he had to agree. The judge's word was law.

The onlookers gave a loud cheer and the horse lived comfortably for the rest of his days, loved and cared for by the kind people of Atri.

Clever Katya

On the vast plains of Russia, lived two brothers. They both bred horses for a living, but one was rich and mean, while the other was poor and kind. Every October, there was a huge horse market in the nearest town, so the two brothers set off together, the rich brother on his strong, sleek stallion and the poor brother on his fat, little mare.

It was many miles to the town, so they stopped for the night on the way, leaving their horses in a small field outside the hut where they were staying. Exhausted after a long day on the road, they soon fell fast asleep.

Imagine their surprise the following morning when, outside the hut, they found three horses instead of two. The third horse was a newborn foal. The shy creature was only just able to stand up on its unsteady legs, and was sheltering beside the sturdy legs of the stallion.

"It looks like I have a new horse!" announced Dimitri, the rich brother.

"How could a stallion give birth to a foal?" laughed Leo, the poor brother. "My mare gave birth to the foal, so it belongs to me."

"It's standing next to my stallion, so the foal must be mine. Stop arguing with me!" snapped back Dimitri.

"You're crazy, but if you really insist, let's take the matter to the judge in the town. He will soon put an end to your foolish ideas," Leo replied.

The two men kept up their arguing all the way to town. When they arrived, the town was bustling with crowds. Every kind of horse was there, from pretty palominos to enormous carthorses. It was a special day. Not only was it the annual horse market, but the emperor himself was visiting. Today, he would hear all problems and decide what was to be done, instead of the local judge.

The two brothers made their way to the courthouse in the main square and found themselves in front of the emperor. Slightly in awe, they told him about their dispute.

The emperor tried not to laugh. "This must be the silliest case I have ever heard," he thought. He looked from one brother to the other. Of course he knew the foal belonged to Leo, but he decided to have some fun with the

brothers. He listened carefully to each of their stories and then he nodded.

"Hmm, I can see both your points of view," he pretended. "The only way for me to decide is to ask you these four riddles. Whoever can solve them, can keep the foal. What is the fastest thing in the world? What is the fattest? What is the softest? And what is the most precious? I will return in one week to hear your answers!" And, with that, he moved on to the next case.

Dimitri puzzled over the riddles all the way home, but failed to come up with any solution. He needed help, but he had no friends he could ask. Then he remembered a woman he'd once loaned some money to. She seemed a clever sort, maybe she could help him.

The woman was certainly cunning, as she quickly demanded he wipe out all her debt in return for her answer.

"The fastest thing in the world," she said, "is my husband's racehorse. The fattest is our huge pig. The softest is my feather quilt. And the most precious thing is my baby nephew."

These answers did not sound quite right to Dimitri, but he had no one else to ask, so he accepted them with a shrug and wrote off her debt.

Leo also knew he could never solve the riddles by himself. He went back to the tiny cottage, where he lived as a widower with his seven-year-old daughter, Katya. She was a thoughtful little girl and Leo shared his problem with her.

She considered for a moment, then told him, "The fastest thing in the world is the north wind. The fattest is the soil which gives us our food. The softest is a child's kiss. And the most precious thing is honesty."

The brothers made their way back to the town, and once more they found themselves before the emperor. Dimitri gave his answers first. The emperor howled with laughter at such foolishness.

Next was Leo's turn. The emperor prepared himself for more amusement, but his grin soon turned to a frown. He knew Leo was right and felt ashamed. Honesty *was* precious and he had not been honest with the brothers. He could not admit that in front of the court though.

"You have given me the right answers," he told Leo, "so you shall keep the foal and take one hundred silver ducats too. But tell me, did you come up with these answers yourself, or did somebody help you?"

"My daughter Katya gave me the answers," replied Leo, displaying his honesty.

"If you have such a clever daughter, I would like to meet her. Bring her to court and tell her to solve this riddle: she must be neither on foot nor on horseback, and neither bearing gifts nor empty-handed. If she can do this, you can keep the foal and the silver ducats. If she fails, you shall forfeit both!"

Poor Leo didn't see how Katya could manage that. But he went home and told her what the emperor had said.

"Don't worry, Father," she told him calmly. "Go out and catch a hare and a partridge. Bring them both back alive."

Leo had no idea how this could possibly help, but he trusted her and took her advice. The next day, they set off to town with the hare, the partridge and the foal.

The courthouse was packed with onlookers, all waiting to see how Katya would solve the riddle. When Katya appeared, she was riding the hare and holding the partridge in her hand. The crowd gasped at such a strange sight.

The emperor looked curiously at Katya for a

moment, then boomed, "I said not bearing gifts nor empty-handed!"

Katya held out the partridge. The emperor reached to take it, but the bird flapped its wings and flew off.

The emperor had to admit this little girl was clever.

"You win!" he said. "Your father can keep the foal and the hundred silver ducats. Just answer me this, is he really as poor as he looks?"

"Oh yes," replied Katya, "we live on the hares he catches in the river and the fish he picks from the trees."

"What do you mean? Whoever heard of hares in the river and fish in the trees?"

Quick as a flash, Katya replied, "Whoever heard of a stallion giving birth to a foal?"

The emperor burst out laughing. He liked clever Katya.

"Only in my kingdom could such a clever little girl be born!" he declared with pride, as Katya led the foal home in triumph.

About the Stories

$\mathcal{P}$eople have been living with horses and ponies, and telling stories about them, since horses were first tamed about 6,000 years ago. So it's not surprising many traditional tales feature horses.

Here, you can find out a little more about the tales which inspired this collection.

The Talking Horse – a fairytale from Germany, collected by the Brothers Grimm; their version was called *The Goose Girl*

Bronze, Silver and Gold – a fairytale from Norway

The Black Stallion – a fairytale from Greece

The Little Humpbacked Pony – an old Russian fairytale, told in a poem by Pyotr Yershov

The Kelpie – a folktale from Scotland

Ivan and the Chestnut Horse – a fairytale from Russia

The Magician's Horse – a story from the Middle East, from a collection known as *The Arabian Nights*

Dapplebright – a fairytale from Norway, also known as *Dapplegrim*

The White Mare – a fairytale from Italy, from a collection known as *The Pentamerone*

The Seven Foals – a fairytale from Norway

The Princess and the Unicorn – a modern English fairytale

The Good~Luck Horse – a folktale from China

The First Horses – an ancient Greek myth

The Horse, the Fox and the Lion – an ancient fable attributed to a Greek storyteller named Aesop

Pegasus – an ancient Greek myth, told in a poem by Friedrich von Schiller

The Old Horse of Atri – a folktale from Italy

Clever Katya – a folktale from Russia; similar tales are told across Europe

Designed by: Lenka Hrehova

Digital manipulation: Nick Wakeford

Edited by Rosie Dickins and Lesley Sims

First published in 2017 by Usborne Publishing Ltd.,
83-85 Saffron Hill, London EC1N 8RT, England. www.usborne.com
Copyright © 2017 Usborne Publishing Limited.
The name Usborne and the devices ♀⬤ are Trade Marks
of Usborne Publishing Ltd. All rights reserved.

First published in America in 2017. UE.